FIRE

OF THE SKY

MADALYN RAE

For my readers. Without you, none of this would be possible. To the budding authors out there, you can do it. The best way to start is to start.

WHAT TO EXPECT

I'm not one to give trigger warnings, however, I think this book might need a few. Please be aware there are mentions of death, abandonment, starvation, emaciation, and torture. Adria's journey to find the love of her life is a harrowing one that will leave you confused, frustrated, fulfilled, and furious or a combination of all of the above.

CHAPTER 1

*O*ne month.

Four weeks.

Twenty-eight days.

Seven hundred and thirty hours.

That's how much time has passed since *my* world stopped, while life around me continues as if nothing has happened. As if the man I love, more than life itself, wasn't kidnapped by Vita, the Goddess of Aether, and being held somewhere out of my reach.

My father, Llyr, the God of Water, has been gone exactly four days longer. Murdered in front of me, while I did nothing but watch. Two of the most important men in my life—gone in the blink of an eye.

"Adria?" I recognize the voice of my grandfather as he knocks on my door. "Why don't you come downstairs for a while?" I don't answer. "You can't stay up here, locked in your room forever. Hell, never mind." I feel the energy shift as he appears in my room, surpassing the door altogether. "Oh, dear gods. What's this?" He points to my baggy sweatpants, oversized hoodie, and greasy hair.

Shu, the God of Air, who also happens to be my grandfather, looks fabulous as always. His signature white jeans and sequin white sweater are perfectly creased and flawless. "It's called, I don't give a shit."

"Hmph," he grunts as a blast of wind picks me up and carries me into the bathroom. "Well, you certainly smell like it." He moves in front of me, turning the shower on. "You aren't doing him any good, sitting up here, sulking, feeling sorry for yourself, and smelling like that." He walks out of my closet, carrying a pair of jeans and a cotton shirt. "Take a shower, get dressed, and brush that rat's nest on your head. Everyone's downstairs with the latest news."

"I don't want to," I whisper.

"Sometimes we have to do things we don't want to do. This is one of those times. You've been through one hell of a ride, but it's not over. We're in halftime, and the band has just finished marching. It's time to get out there and find that man. Llyr's gone, but Murphy's not." He looks around at the mess I've created.

"You're being an asshole," I murmur.

"I prefer to call it tough love." He pulls the bathroom door closed behind him. "If you're not downstairs smelling better in thirty minutes, I'm coming in there after you."

"You wouldn't dare!" I yell through the door.

"Oh, I would definitely dare." He pauses. "Twenty-nine minutes and counting."

The main door closes, echoing through the bathroom. Sometimes I don't like him. But, as much as I hate to admit it, he's right. I'm not doing Murphy any good by hiding in this room. The water is rejuvenating as it streams over my tired muscles. Sitting around and sulking is exhausting.

Four washes later, my hair has lost the gooey feel and regained its curl. "Thirteen minutes," Shu says, standing on the other side of the shower curtain.

"Thank you, Father Time." I hear him chuckle as his energy disappears. Dressing in the outfit he laid out, I pull my hair into a bun, slip on a pair of Converse, and leave my room for the first time in a week.

"There she is!" Shu exclaims as I enter the office. "And with two minutes to spare." He hugs me, pulling me close. "It's good to see you."

"Your Highness." Tempest, my favorite water elemental, bows his head. "It's good to see you again."

Keegan, my security chief, stands, moving closer. "We have some news." He takes my hand, pulling me to a chair.

"You found him?" My voice breaks with my words.

"Not quite," Tempest answers. "But we've narrowed down possible places he could be."

"Based on what you saw when you projected to his holding cell and reading through hours of Ethan's books about elementals, we've narrowed his possible locations down to three." Keegan leans against the side of the desk.

"What are you saying?" I ask, looking at each person in the room.

"They're saying, while you were upstairs, feeling sorry for yourself, they've been working their asses off to find Murphy." Shu never has been one to mince words.

Although his black hair is longer than I remember,

and his eyes look tired, Keegan has a smile on his face. Tempest's hair is messy for the first time since I've known him, and he has small bags under his bright green eyes.

"You two have been working on this the entire time?"

"Sophie, Ethan, and Shu helped, too," Tempest answers.

"I don't know what to say," I admit.

"I believe thank you would be in order," Shu answers for me.

I look each of them in the eyes. "Thank you," I whisper. "I'm sorry I wasn't here to help you."

"You're here now." Tempest smiles. "Now it's your turn. We've gone as far as we can without you."

"How do we know these locations aren't going to be like the hundreds we've checked before?"

Shu pulls a chair out for me, motioning to the seat. "Those first places we visited were part of Vita's plan. She's been playing me for centuries, all leading up to this insane plot of hers to control every element. Her plan has been in the works for who knows how long."

"What are you saying?"

"I'm saying that bitch has led me on a wild goose chase and is probably laughing about it as we speak." He sits beside me.

"Do you have a plan?" I ask the small group around me.

"There are five of us and three possible locations," Keegan answers.

"No. Absolutely not. It's not safe. I'm the only one powerful enough to fight her." I look at the elementals in front of me. "I won't let you risk your lives like that."

"Adria, we're..."

"No," I interrupt Tempest's protest. "I won't hear any arguments. I'm the Goddess of Air, Earth, Fire, and Water. I'm going to pull rank here and forbid any of you to search for him."

"Don't pull that rank shit on me," Shu reprimands. "I'm not letting you do this alone. We'll go together. I'm not helpless, you know."

Stephen walks into the room, carrying plates of food. "I don't think we're very hungry, Stephen," I say, stopping his trek.

"Speak for yourself," Keegan interrupts. "I'm starving!" Stephen sets the plates in the middle of the table, and Keegan digs in.

"Adria, I've known Murphy since he was a child. If there's anything I can do to help, please let me know." Stephen pauses at the entrance.

"Of course. Thank you." He continues into the kitchen. "So," I look around the room. "Where am I going?"

"You mean, where are we going?" Shu corrects.

Keegan points to a second plate. "Anyone going to eat this?"

"No, have at it," Shu answers.

Tempest scoots back in his chair. "We've ranked the top three locations in order of highest probability to lowest."

"Okay, what's number one?"

"Alabama," Tempest answers.

"Alabama? As in Roll Tide?"

"I have no idea what that means, but Alabama, as in the southern part of the United States," he answers.

"Last time I checked, there were no castles in Alabama. When I saw him, the building felt like a castle."

"There aren't any castles, but there are several old forts on the Gulf Coast that would fit the descriptions you gave. We've found hints in a few of Ethan's books of Vita being at the forts in the past." Keegan stacks his empty plates.

"Ethan found more information on Vita?"

Keegan nods. "He's done nothing but research since... since this happened."

I turn to Shu. "When will the plane be ready?"

He wrinkles his forehead. "We don't need the plane. We can be there in a blink of an eye." I nod, understanding.

"Without an energy signature to grab onto, I can't get us there."

"No, but I can." Shu wiggles his eyebrows. "I've been to each location several times. I can get us there. However, I think it's better for you to wear your gear. I'll do the same. I have no idea what we're going to run into when we arrive, but it's better to be safe than sorry. Plus, we'll look fabulous when we get there."

I notice Keegan's face light up as Sophie enters the room. "You're here!" she exclaims, wrapping her arms around my waist. "Have they filled you in on what we've discovered?"

"Yes. Shu and I are leaving for Alabama in a moment." I wrap my arm around hers. "How are Bonnie and Ethan holding up?"

She sighs. "Mom spends a lot of time crying. She tries to hide it from me, but I hear her. Dad's been buried in books since Murphy's been...gone. He's searching day and night for clues."

"How are you?"

"Good. Keegan's kept me busy." Keegan smiles at his name. Normally, I would take that little sliver of information and run with it, but now isn't the time to tease them about a possible relationship.

"I'll meet you back down here in ten minutes," Shu announces, moving toward the stairs.

True to his word, he's waiting for me at the bottom of the stairs, wearing his version of fighting gear, when I return. Where mine is black and resembles a leather version of medieval knight's armor, his is lightweight, white, and, of course, stylish.

"I'll know within minutes if he's there." I move to his side. "We won't need to stay long."

"Good. Ready?" He kisses me on the forehead. I nod, and together, we blink out of existence and onto bright green grass and cerulean, blue skies. Warm sea air hits me instantly as we take a minute to study our surroundings. We're in the middle of the fort, surrounded by tall brick walls and empty arched rooms.

"Are we in Alabama?"

"Feels more like hell. I'm already sweating," Shu answers, fanning himself. A family with two children walks past us, staring. I try not to laugh, thinking about what we must look like to them.

"Are they doing some sort of reenactment today?" the mother asks, pointing at our training gear.

"I don't think those are uniforms that would have been worn during the time this fort was in use," the man answers, ushering his family away.

"Are they aliens?" a young girl asks as the family moves quickly. A chorus of hushes follows her words.

"Do you feel anything?" Shu asks.

I send my energy through the ruins—feeling inside each corridor, each ancient building, each hidden area, but finding nothing. "No, nothing familiar. I do feel something. There's a strange energy here." Shu looks up in question.

"Oh, that's just the ghosts," an older woman says from behind. "I'm sorry, I was eavesdropping. I have a bad habit of doing that." She moves closer. "You're standing in the middle of one of the most haunted sites in Alabama. If y'all feel something weird, it's all those ghosts that are wandering about, still trying to fight in the war." She drags out the endings of her words, making her sound like the epitome of a Southern Belle.

"That's our cue to go," Shu says, opening his eyes wide. "No Murphy?" I shake my head. He turns to the ghost lady. "Excuse me, ma'am. We didn't realize anyone could see us. It's been a long time since we've had anyone alive talk to us, you know, being ghosts and all." He nudges my hand, and we jump out of the fort and back to the castle.

"You just gave that woman a heart attack." I smile for the first time in a while.

"Ah, you do remember how to smile. I was beginning to think those muscles had broken." He smirks, making me want to slap him and hug him at the same time.

"Maybe not a heart attack, but certainly something to talk about at her next book club meeting." He pats my shoulder.

"What happened?" Sophie asks, standing from the table the moment we return.

"He wasn't there," I answer.

"Dammit, I really thought that was our best choice." Keegan crosses his arms in front of his chest.

"There was nothing there but tourists and ghost hunters. Where do we go next?"

"China," Tempest answers. "There's a temple that was built centuries ago in honor of the fifth element."

"They worship Vita?" I ask the group.

"Not really, and don't let her hear you say that. Her ego is big enough as it is," Shu answers. "Over the millennia humans have been on earth, each of the Firsts have had groups of humans who have revered us, almost worshiped us. This temple was built in honor of the source of all light and love in the universe."

I laugh at the irony. "Light and love, my ass. Let's go."

Like before, we jump straight into the middle of our location, a large hall. Beautiful pillars line the walkway, each at least thirty feet tall. The ceiling is covered with intricately painted tiles, the bright colors, offsetting the ebony floors. At the front of the room is a statue of a tall man. He's wearing traditional Chinese clothing, and his hair is tied tightly behind his head. "This is beautiful," I whisper, rubbing my hand along the arm of the statue.

"Yes, it is. That's what they think Vita looks like."

I can't control my laugh. "I like this version better."

"Feel anything?" Shu looks around nervously. Just like

the fort, I release my energy throughout the building, searching every corner and hall throughout the temple.

"No," I answer. "I don't feel Murphy, but what's even more strange is I don't feel anyone at all. No human energy, nothing."

"I'm ready if you are," Shu says. "This place gives me the creeps." We return to the dining room and our awaiting audience. They all stand as we return.

"Nothing." I cut their questions short. "Where to next?"

Keegan grabs a notebook from the table, flipping through a few pages. "Jordan. Petra, to be exact."

"Isn't that the treasury that was carved into the side of a mountain?"

"It is. Let's go," Shu answers. We jump to the front of the treasury, surrounded by hundreds of tourists and dozens of charter buses. "Well, this one won't be discreet. Follow me." We head toward the front of the mountain.

An older man approaches us, carrying a tray of shiny trinkets and tourist traps. "Jewelry for the lady?" His accent is thick, making it difficult to understand his words.

"No, thank you," I answer.

He steps in front of us, blocking our movement. "I'll make you a great deal."

"The lady said no, thank you." Shu and I continue moving. The man moves in front of us again. A blast of air picks him up, setting him down in front of a group of older American tourists unloading from a bus. The man doesn't question what happened, just continues peddling his wares. "Let's get inside before we're forced to either buy something or kill him."

A guard steps in front of us. "Not open." His broken English is hard to understand.

Shu sighs. "Do your thing."

I send energy through the building, through the surrounding mountains, and into the maze of tunnels below. My legs buckle the moment I feel him. "He's here or was here. His energy is below us."

The guard at the door is picked up and moved to the other side of the building by a blast of rogue wind. "Oh, look. It's open." I follow Shu inside.

CHAPTER 2

The room we enter is large and plain compared to the touristy area out front and at the entrance of the treasury. Our boots echo around the stone-covered walls with each step. "Do you still feel him?"

I nod, searching for an exit. Narrow archways lead away from this room, each ending in a smaller version of the first. Both of those rooms are completely bare. Nothing more than stone walls carved into the limestone bedrock.

"These rooms are a dead end. He's underneath, but how the hell do we get there?" My hand engulfs in flames, filling the darkened rooms with light.

"You're thinking like a human, my dear. Can you lock into his energy?"

I focus on Murphy. Feeling his faint pull below our feet. "Yes."

"Take us to that energy." Shu wraps his thin fingers through mine. "Think like the goddess you are."

Pulling on the energy of our connection and my love for Murphy, I focus all of my energy on locating his signal. Instantly, we're transported to a room deep within the tunnels beneath the facade. The smell of death is the same as I remember from my vision. "This is it. This is where I saw him." The room is small, and it takes only seconds to realize it's empty. Just like my vision, a pile of rotting rat corpses is stacked next to a pile of rotten hay.

"Shit!" I scream. My voice ricochets off the limestone. "It took this long to find his energy, and he's gone!" I kick the wall, knocking a boot-sized hole through the stone. "He's running out of time. We can't keep playing these games."

"This is good news," Shu says, pissing me off even more.

"Please explain how this is good?"

"Adria, he was here. You found him by using your abilities. You will do it again." Shu walks around the small room. "Murphy's smart. Look for anything out of the ordinary. Maybe he left a clue."

"This whole damn room is out of the ordinary." I light several small fires throughout the space, filling the room with light. Tears fill my eyes, thinking about him living in this shithole for a month. The pile of hay in the back corner looks more like a nest than a bed. Sorting through it, I don't find any clues. "Nothing over here."

"Why would he stack these rats?" Shu points at the carcasses thrown on top of each other.

"Food, maybe?" I push that thought from my mind. If he resorted to eating raw rat meat...

"Look at this." Thankfully, Shu interrupts my thoughts. "There are some scratches on the stone over here."

I run my fingers over the scratches. "It looks like letters of some sort, but I don't recognize the language." Running my fingers along the carving, "A′ Ghrèig," I say each letter separately.

"What does that mean?"

"I have no idea. You're older than humans, don't you speak their languages?"

He wrinkles his forehead. "Most of my time has been spent staying away from humans. I have better things to do with my time than to learn all of their languages."

"Ethan will know." I take a quick picture of the scratches. "Do you see anything else?"

"No, that's it."

I take one last look around the room. "Shu, if he was trapped in here..."

"Don't go there. He's strong, Adria. If anyone can survive, it's Murphy." We jump back to the dining room where Tempest is the only one remaining.

"We found something," I say, pulling my phone out of my vest pocket. "Where are Keegan and Sophie?"

"They went back to the apartment for more research."

"That's perfect. Ethan's just the person we need to see." Tempest joins me, heading to the door.

"I'll meet you there." Shu's standing at the brandy cart with a full glass in hand.

"Shall I meet you there, too?" Tempest stops by the door.

"No. I'll walk with you. I could use some fresh air. A few minutes isn't going to change the course of things." Tempest falls in step with me as we cross the old bridge, heading toward the village.

"I haven't told you how much I appreciate everything you've done for Llyr, me, Murphy, and your element. You've been someone I can depend on, no matter the quest."

"I don't know how to respond to that," Tempest says as we enter the outskirts of the village.

"You don't have to respond. I just want you to know how much I appreciate you." I wrap my arm through his, feeling him tense on contact. "I'm sorry, I should have asked before touching you."

He smiles, wrapping my arm back through his. "When you spend most of your life in the sea, physical contact can be foreign at times." The fountain and small bookstore come into view. Tempest's water energy reminds me of Llyr, and I'm grateful for the brief connection to my father.

"Did you find anything?" Keegan asks the moment we enter the upstairs apartment. Shu enters behind us like he's been there the entire time.

"He was there," I answer. Bonnie comes around the corner from the kitchen. She's searching the space around me, looking for her son.

"You found him? Where is he?" She wipes wet hands on her apron.

"Gone. But he had been there." Bonnie clutches her chest as Sophie directs her to the couch.

"What does that mean?" Sophie asks.

"It means Vita moved him," Shu says, sitting next to Bonnie.

"We found scratches on the wall where he was being held. I think it's a word, but neither of us recognized the language. I thought Ethan might be able to translate it."

"Show me," Ethan says, taking my phone. "It's Gaelic," he announces seconds later.

"What's it say, Dad?" Sophie asks.

"A' Ghrèig."

"Greece? What does that mean?" she asks.

Shu stands. "That word means Greece? As in the country of Greece?"

"Yes. Dad taught Murphy and me languages from around the UK. Scottish Gaelic was one of many."

"What are the chances of finding Gaelic words written on a wall in Jordan?" I ask.

"I would say, none to none," Shu answers as Ethan moves to the bookshelf, pulling a book from a high shelf. "Ethan?"

He holds up a finger, flipping through the tattered book. The pages are brown with age and the once complete cover is torn and frayed on the edges. "I read something about an island in Greece earlier today." He pauses, flipping through the pages quickly. "Here, here it is." He points to a line in the book. "The source of all finds respite in Crete." He looks up. "Crete is the oldest inhabited island in Greece. It would make sense."

"Have you visited Vita in Greece?" I ask Shu.

"No. I've been to Crete many times throughout the millennia, however. The islands are some of the most beautiful on earth."

Bonnie moves next to me. "Adria, do you think he's okay? Is he...alive?"

I put my hand over hers. "I do. He's strong."

"Can you pinpoint his energy?" Keegan asks.

"I've tried. Countless times. I keep hitting a wall. It's like his energy is being hidden from me."

"The same way Brenna hides her energy?" he asks. "Since she's the first elemental to be able to mask her energy, maybe she knows how to unmask energy."

Brenna, the first created lesser fire elemental, has been on Earth almost as long as the First Elementals. "Keegan, you're a genius!" I give him a quick hug before jumping straight to the fire castle in Iceland.

"Brenna!" I call through the empty halls. The furniture is covered with white sheets, making the castle look abandoned. "Brenna? Rhys? Is anyone here?" My voice echoes through the halls.

"Adria?" I run toward my fire office and the familiar voice.

"Rhys?" I find him inside, lying in a pool of dried blood. "Oh, my gods. Rhys! What happened?"

His eyes flash wildly, searching every corner of the room. "Someone was here." His voice is harsh and scratchy.

"Where's Brenna?"

He coughs before answering. "I don't know. I haven't seen her since...since," his words are cut short by an even stronger cough.

"Rhys. I'm so sorry. When did this happen?" From the looks of the clotted blood surrounding him, a few days have passed.

"I've watched the sun set a few times."

"Let me help you up." He groans as soon as I try to move him.

"It's no use. I've tried. My back is broken and not healing." He grabs my shoulder. "Thank you for coming back. I thought I would die alone."

"I'm not going to let that happen." I shove a small pillow under his head, and he winces with the pain. "Do you know what happened?"

"I was in the kitchen when I heard Brenna scream. There was a man. He hit me." He coughs, this time spewing blood on the side of his face. "I let him get the best of me, Adria. I'm sorry I let you down. I let Brenna down."

"Rhys, this isn't your fault. You didn't let anyone down. What did the man that did this to you look like?" I already know the answer.

"He was tall with dark hair and was wearing a black hat and coat." That description only fits one person, Lucian. Why would he come here? He had to know I wasn't on the island. What could he have wanted with Brenna and Rhys?

"I'm going to take you with me."

He holds his hand up. "No, this is where I belong."

"You belong with people who love you. I'm going to take you to someone who can help."

"What about Brenna?" he asks, a tear sliding down his cheek. "She's all I have..." He doesn't finish his thought.

"Allowing yourself to die on this floor, alone, is not what she would want for you. We'll find her," I promise. "Close your eyes." Rhys reluctantly follows directions, and I wipe the tear from his cheek. Putting my hand on his, I transport the two of us to the Isle of Man and back to the apartment I left moments earlier.

"Is that Rhys?" Keegan asks as we appear on the floor.

"He's injured. He needs help." Bonnie jumps into action at my words, wiping the blood from Rhys's face.

"Sophie, bring me a bowl of water. Tempest, carry him to the bedroom and put him on Murphy's bed." Both jump at her orders.

"I'm guessing Brenna was nowhere to be found when you got there," Shu says.

"How'd you know?"

"Oh, just a hunch."

I wipe the blood from my hand with the towel left on the floor. "You don't think Brenna had anything to do with all this, do you?"

"There's *no* way Brenna had *anything* to do with this," Keegan interrupts. "She's rough around the edges, but she would never betray you, Adria. Whoever did this to Rhys has her."

"Did he say what happened?" Shu nods in the direction of Rhys.

"He's a little confused, but he gave me a description of the person that did this to him."

"Lucian?" Shu confirms. I nod in response.

Ethan, who's kept his nose buried in a book the entire time, looks up at our words. "Lucian? Is that his name? Vita's child is named Lucian?"

"Aye, and he's the hat man," Sophie adds, passing through the sitting room with water for Bonnie. "The one from my dreams."

"Aye, I remember you having those dreams as a child." He looks at me, eyes wide-open. "Lucian is the one who stalks humans, giving them nightmares?"

"Sophie thinks so. The description certainly fits," I answer.

"Have you seen him? I mean other than in a dream?" Ethan pulls out a different book. This one is older than the first and much larger. "There are records of the hat man throughout history." He flips to an old sketch, turning it for everyone to see. His face looks a little different, but it's definitely Lucian.

"That's him." I take the book from Ethan. "How old is this?"

"That copy is five hundred years old. However, it's a reprint from a book that's been around since medieval times."

"You think Lucian has been in existence for over a thousand years?" Shu asks.

"Possibly longer," Ethan answers.

"What does all this have to do with Murphy or Brenna?" Keegan asks. "Why would he take her? It doesn't make sense."

"Nothing that bitch does makes any sense," Shu answers. "Even if Lucian took Brenna on his own account, I guarantee Vita had her hand in it."

Bonnie comes back to the living room. "He's weak but alive. His back is broken, but I can't find any wounds that would have caused all the blood that covers him."

"Could it be someone else's blood?" Keegan asks.

"Aye, it could," she answers.

Keegan sits quickly. "Brenna." He lays his head in his hands. "What if she's..."

"She's not," I interrupt. "You've known her a lot longer than I have, but one thing I learned is that she's not going down without a fight. She's the strongest lesser I know."

"Then why take her?" he repeats.

"Maybe she wasn't taken. Maybe she's tracking them?" Shu slides to the front of the couch.

"Could she do that?"

"If anyone could, it would be her," Shu answers.

"Then we have to find her," Keegan announces. "If she's bleeding that much, she's hurt and needs our help."

"She could be anywhere. She's strong and should have healed by now. If she needs our help, she'll come to us. Right now, we need to focus on finding Murphy." Shu stands from the couch. "Adria, I think your time right now is better spent at the castle. You need to work on finding his energy and following it."

Shu has never been the parental type. The sharpness of his tone tells me he has other things on his mind. I don't argue, and together, we jump back to the castle and back in Llyr's old office.

"I've tried finding his energy for a month. I've tried every second of every day since she took him. What work do you think I can do that will make that easier? I've fully stepped into my powers. If I were able to find him, I would have found him by now." My words sound as frustrated as I am.

"I know. I apologize, but I needed to get you alone." Shu motions to the couch. "Sit, please." I've rarely seen Shu serious about any topic. I sit without argument. "I haven't been completely honest with you." Energy rises in my core. "Before you release those killer death blows you've got charging, let me explain."

I take a deep breath. "In my experience, when someone prefaces a conversation with those words, it's not good news."

Shu doesn't have any witty comebacks, no smart aleck comments. Instead, he lowers his head, almost in submission. "I wasn't honest about mine and Vita's relationship." He rubs a hand through his hair, looking more human than ever. His hair is disheveled for the first time since I've known him. "Vita and I had a *relationship* many millennia ago."

My eyes feel as large as saucers. "Define relationship."

"A relationship. You know, consensual sex between two consenting adults."

"I thought you weren't a fan of women." I stumble over my words.

He smiles. "I have my moments."

"How long did it last?"

"A few thousand years or so," he answers.

I slide forward on the couch, scared to ask the question I need to know. "Shu, can two gods produce a child?"

He looks down and sighs before answering. "I don't know."

I walk to the closest window. "Dammit, Shu. Is there a possibility that Lucian's your son?" He doesn't respond. "Shu?"

"Yes."

"How could you keep this from me?"

He shrugs. "To be honest, I didn't think it was important."

"Not important?" I echo. "You had a relationship with the Goddess of Aether? The same Goddess of Aether who wants nothing more than to kill all of the Firsts and gain their powers. The fact that you possibly fathered a child with her didn't seem 'important'?" I use air quotes.

He steps toward the bar cart, filling a glass to the brim. "I didn't think it was possible to produce a child. I'm still not convinced."

"Did you leave her while she was pregnant?"

He shakes his head. "I had no idea she had a child until Ethan found it in that book."

"Gods dammit, Shu. That would explain why he's so strong." I take the glass of brandy from him, drinking half of it.

Shu stares at me, without speaking. "Adria, I'm sorry. I have to go." He disappears from the room.

CHAPTER 3

I jump back to the apartment and my friends.
"What's going on?" Keegan rushes to my side
the instant I arrive. "Shu was acting weird. I mean, he
always acts weird, but he was weird, even for him."

"He's gone, and I don't know when or if he'll be
back." I don't elaborate or give Keegan time to ask more
questions. "Ethan? Do you have any possible locations
for Vita's home in Crete?" He scurries to a different
book.

"Here." He points to a map.

"What are we looking at?" I pull the book out of his
hands.

"I don't think she's on the actual island of Crete
anymore. Humans have taken over the island, and she
doesn't seem like the type that would entertain them." He
points to a smaller island further south. "This is where I
believe she is or at least was."

"Gavdos." I read the small print.

"What makes you so sure, Dad?" Sophie looks over her father's shoulder.

We watch in silence as Ethan pulls out a second book. "There are mentions of Gavdos throughout time in several different historical texts. Call it a gut feeling, I guess."

"Gut feelings are better than nothing," Tempest adds and turns toward me. "If Shu's gone, you don't need to jump to the island alone."

I cross my arms defiantly. "If Murphy's there, I'm not making him wait another minute."

"In elemental form, I can be there in a few hours. Do us both a favor, and wait for me." His voice echoes off the walls of the small apartment.

"Aye, he's right," Bonnie chimes in. "You don't know what you're going to be walking into. From what you all have said, she's not going to be very welcoming. Wait on Tempest." Her voice is sad, yet sincere.

Dammit. As much as I'd like to try, this is something I can't do alone. "I'm the Goddess of Water. I'll swim with you."

Tempest smiles. "I like that idea."

"Excuse me," Keegan says, raising his hand. "I will not sit idly by and watch the two of you swim away into the sunset to rescue Murphy and hopefully Brenna, with me waving in the background."

"You're a fire hybrid, Keegan," Sophie says. "You can't swim."

"No, but I can fly," he answers with a smile.

"Aye. I'll call Daniel." She pulls her phone out of her pocket and steps into the kitchen.

"We'll get there before you." Tempest crosses his arms across his chest.

"You're going to have to wait on me," he answers. "If Brenna's there, she needs help. I won't sit here twiddling my thumbs waiting for you to return." Tempest looks at me for confirmation.

"We'll wait on you," I answer.

"Good, you'll wait on me too. Daniel will have the plane ready in twenty minutes." Sophie walks back into the room.

"If you two insist on going, we should stay together. We'll all ride on the plane. We'll need it to get them home anyway. Murphy's not going to be in any position to swim." My heart wants to get to him now, but common sense wins out.

"We're like the Fantastic Four," Keegan says, sticking his hand in the middle of our small circle. "Come on, stack your hands on top."

"No," Tempest answers, walking toward the door.

"Pack a bag, and I'll meet you all at the airport," I announce before jumping straight to my room at the castle. Stephen, Llyr's and now my butler, has already cleaned my weeks of filth, making the bedroom beautiful again. I grab a backpack from the closet, shoving a few clothing items inside. Tempest was right. I have no idea what we'll be walking into. We could be there for an hour, a week, or a month. I don't know.

"The plane is ready," Stephen says, knocking lightly on the door. "I'll drive you to the airport. The rest are on their way there now."

"Thank you. I'll be right there." Heading into

Murphy's room, I grab a clean set of his clothes and shove them next to mine. Ten minutes later, Stephen pulls onto the tarmac and to the awaiting jet. The rest of the Fantastic Four are waiting next to the stairs. Each is carrying a small backpack similar to mine.

"I've taken the liberty to pack some food," Stephen says, handing me a second backpack as we approach the group.

"Oh, thank gods," Keegan says. "I'm starving."

"Thank you, Stephen." I take the backpack, and the four of us run onto the plane.

"Our departure has already been cleared. Please secure all belongings. We will be taking off momentarily," Daniel's voice booms over the speaker. The plane begins to taxi, and we're off the ground minutes later.

"Delta Airlines needs to take lessons from Daniel," Keegan announces a few minutes into the flight. "He knows how to get things done."

"What's the plan?" Tempest asks once we're off the ground.

"There isn't one," I answer truthfully. "I'll be able to tell if he's there within seconds of arriving."

"I'll stay with Daniel when we land, while the three of you search." Sophie unstraps her seatbelt the moment the light goes off.

"You're not coming with us?" Keegan asks.

"I'm of better use here, on the plane. Down there, I'd only get in the way." Keegan nods in understanding.

"What if Murphy's energy is hidden?" Keegan asks. "When you were in the catacombs, you said his energy was masked when Lucian was inside him."

"True. But from the condition Murphy was in during my vision, I don't think Lucian's inside." I look at my makeshift family. "If he's there, I need to get him, alone."

"That's not..." Tempest starts.

"No," I interrupt. "I can get in and get him out in the blink of an eye. You'll only be dead weight." Tempest wrinkles his forehead in frustration at my words. "If he's there, I'll bring him back to the plane."

"What if you run into Vita or Lucian in there? You won't be able to fight them and take care of Murphy, too. Think this through, Your Highness. This is the reason we came. I will protect you with my life."

"I know you will, and I have thought this through. If he's there, my focus is getting him out. I won't engage in a fight," I answer.

"What if you aren't given a choice?" Keegan retorts.

"That's a chance I'm willing to take. You're staying here." Both men sigh and reluctantly nod in agreement. Neither speaks much for the remainder of the trip.

"Ladies and gentlemen," Daniel announces several hours later. "We're approaching the landing strip in Gavdos. Please put on your seatbelts and prepare for a rough landing. This airstrip is not built for a jet of our size."

"What does that mean?" Keegan asks.

"It means, strap in and hold on," Tempest answers. "I don't have to worry about plane crashes when I'm swimming." He mumbles a few choice words under his breath as he follows Daniel's instructions.

Through the window, the small island comes into view.

"The visible land is smaller than a normal runway." The island looks more like the top of a volcano than an inhabitable piece of land. High cliffs, slicing straight through rock, line each of the four sides, topped with a dark green patch of grass. I tighten the seatbelt around me, gripping the armrests. Within seconds, the narrow landing strip comes into view. Instead of concrete, it's nothing more than grass and sand. "Shit," I whisper, closing my eyes.

As soon as the wheels touch down, the plane instantly nose dives. Everything not strapped down is thrown around the cabin. "We're not going to make it!" Sophie yells. "There's not enough room to stop." The jets fire down, as the plane slows even more, but still moving too fast for the strip. "Adria! Do something!"

I jump from my seat to outside the plane, inches in front of the nose. Sophie was right, there's not enough island remaining to come to a complete stop. Through the glass, I see Daniel fighting the wheel with all his strength. Moving to the end of the island, I send a wall of air toward the nose, pushing against the motion. I refuse to let it fall into the Mediterranean Sea.

Using the power of earth, I command the landing strip to lengthen another one hundred yards, allowing more space to stop. With the combination of new ground and air pushing against it, the jet continues to slow, eventually no faster than a roll, before coming to a complete stop. The nose hangs over the side of a cliff, while the front tire is a few feet from the edge.

With one last blast of air, I push the plane away from the edge, and Daniel visibly sighs, closing his eyes in relief.

"Thank you," he mouths through the glass. If he didn't know about elementals before, he does now.

The door swings open and steps drop down. Keegan is the first out. "Oh, my gods. I've never been so happy to see land before." He falls to his knees, kissing the ground.

"Dramatic much?" Sophie steps out behind him.

"Only when I'm about to die."

"That was fun," Tempest says, following Sophie. "I'm swimming home."

Daniel is the last to exit the plane. "Thank you. I knew it was going to be close, but I may have misjudged it a little."

"You think?" Keegan asks.

"Thank you, Daniel. Can you have the plane ready for takeoff soon? I'll make sure there's enough runway."

"Yes, Your Highness." He turns, heading back inside, confirming my suspicions. He's known all along what I am.

"Do you feel anything?" Sophie asks.

I calm my mind and reach for any semblance of Murphy. I send tendrils of energy through each cave, each mountain top, and each tunnel, covering every square inch of the island, until I feel something familiar. I open my eyes to see three sets of eyes staring intently at me. I feel something. I walk away from the edge, closer to the middle of the island, and feel the familiarity again. This time it's stronger but still unidentifiable.

"What is it?" Tempest asks.

"I think I feel him, but he's weak." I fight the tears threatening to fall. Now is not the time for tears. I picture the energy as a rope and follow it until it becomes stronger and easier to locate.

"Can you find the source?" Keegan asks.

Calling on the strength of earth, the calmness of the sea, the wisp of the air, and the ferocity of fire, I pull the four elements into me, using their power to strengthen my senses. I reach for the energy again, this time finding the source. "It's below." I turn to the group standing behind me.

"Can you get to him?" Sophie asks, wiping a tear.

"I think so. Go to the jet. If it's him, we'll take off in minutes. We won't have any time to waste." Surprisingly, they don't argue and follow orders. I make sure they're securely inside before hiding my energy like Brenna taught me and jump to the source of his energy.

Wherever I've jumped gives new meaning to the word dark. There are no differences between my eyes being opened or closed. I don't dare draw attention to myself by producing light. Instead, I focus on bringing light into the space but keeping it contained inside of me. To my surprise, I'm able to see and instantly realize I'm inside what looks like a cave. The walls and ceilings have been carved through solid limestone and look thousands of years old.

I focus on the energy that called me here. It's stronger than before but still weak. The smell of death is overwhelming. Something is or *was* down here. Closing my eyes, I follow the path the energy lays before me until my hand rubs across something not natural, something metallic. A door? I search for a way to open it, finding nothing obvious. No keyhole, no doorknob, nothing.

I can't command the elements making up the steel door but can control the stone surrounding it. Calling on the element of earth, I ask the cave wall to move silently, creating an opening between the wall and the door, and allowing me access inside. The smell that escapes through the newly created opening hits me instantly, along with a familiar, weakened energy.

I float into the room, and it doesn't take long to find the source. My heart stops at what's in front of me. I may be the Goddess of the Four Elements, but at this moment I've never felt more human. Curled into a ball in the back corner of the room is the shell of the man I love. The normally larger-than-life water elemental hybrid that I fell in love with looks small and weak. I rush to his side, resisting the urge to wrap him in my arms.

His eyes are closed, and his breathing is shallow. Without making a sound, I put my hand on his arm. He jumps at the touch, and his eyes open in terror. The Murphy staring back at me looks hollow, empty. "Shh," I hold a finger to my lips, not sure he sees or understands my movement. Without waiting for another second, I jump us both to the jet. We land on the floor, in front of three sets of eyes.

"*Get Brenna,*" Murphy's raspy voice whispers through my mind. His eyes close, and his energy weakens even more.

"Oh, my gods." Sophie runs to her brother and immediately switches into nurse mode.

"Keegan!" I yell. "Brenna's down there. I'm going back." He starts toward the door of the jet without a word.

"No, you stay on the plane. I'll go look for her. Daniel?" I call to the front of the plane. "Get them out of here, now."

"What about Brenna?" Keegan asks, wiping the tears from his eyes. "Adria, we can't leave her here."

"I have no intention of leaving her down there. I'll get her back to the island. I need you to get them home safely." I nod to the rest of the inhabitants.

Tempest and Sophie are working on getting Murphy into one of the seats and strapping him in while I jump out of the jet and back into darkness. I search for her energy, finding nothing. Dammit, Brenna, pull down your shield. Back inside the room where Murphy was, I find the source of the smell from earlier. Dead animals and rotten food line the wall next to the door. Either he was too weak to eat, or someone fed him this shit. I keep my anger at bay, focused on finding Brenna.

Back in the hall, I feel for anything familiar and again am met with nothing. I change tactics. Instead of searching for Brenna, I search for Rhys's energy. They've been together long enough, some of his energy signature could possibly be with her. I'm instantly met with a reward. I feel him not far away. Back into the blackness of the tunnel, I follow the invisible cord to the source and a door identical to Murphy's. Using the same method as before, I ask the wall to shift silently, allowing me access to the room. Once inside, I find the source. Brenna is huddled in a corner, in almost the same condition as Murphy.

She's unconscious and lying in filth. Her skin is ice-cold and clammy. Her heart beats slowly, and her breathing is shallow. A noise in the hallway stops my movement. The sound of shuffling feet sends chills to my core. Whatever is moving this way is breathing. However, their breaths sound more like slow wheezes than actual air entering and exiting. The steps shuffle closer until they stop next to the door.

"Dinner time," the voice says. "It's your favorite, fried rat." The words are followed by a laugh that reminds me of a cartoon character. The door creaks open, and I hold my breath, disguising my body by blending into the stone wall behind me. "Looks like you didn't eat your food yesterday. You must eat, or you won't survive. Even elementals have to eat down here. I'm sorry I can't do better, but rat is better than nothing. It's kept me alive for many years." There's not enough light to see who or what brought her food, but the energy streaming from what-ever it is makes me nervous. The door squeaks as it closes, and the footsteps shuffle away.

"Brenna," I whisper. Her eyes are closed, and she doesn't respond. "Brenna," I repeat. A soft moan escapes her lips. "It's Adria. I'm going to take you to the Isle of Man." She doesn't react, but her energy shield releases and nearly overwhelms me. Dark blood is dried under her nose and on her forehead. Evidence of the source of blood covering Rhys.

"Adria," her weak voice echoes through my mind.

"I'm here," I answer the same way. *"I'm getting you out."* I don't waste another second. Placing my hand on Brenna's shoulder, I jump us back to the water castle and straight to the kitchen where I hope to find Stephen.

"Adria?" Stephen drops the glass he's holding.

"She needs a hospital. Where is the one on the island?"

"Not far from the fountain. I can drive you," he answers, grabbing a set of keys from the wall.

"No, I can get her there faster my way. Can you meet us there? I need to get back to the jet, and I don't want her to be alone."

He nods. "It's the two-story stone building directly behind the bookstore." I jump from the kitchen to the alleyway next to Ethan's bookstore. In front of me stands a stone building that matches Stephen's description.

The door pings as I slam it open. "Miss Smith?" an older gray-haired woman stands from behind a desk. I don't question how she knows who I am.

"She needs help. I don't know the extent of her injuries." Brenna barely weighs anything in my arms. Within minutes, a black SUV pulls in front of the doors. "Her name is Brenna," I tell the woman wearing scrubs.

"I'll get a gurney," she answers, running through a door behind her.

"Go. I'll stay with her." Stephen takes Brenna from my arms. Without responding, I jump back to the jet.

"Adria!" Keegan says, jumping out of his seat. "Did you find her?"

"Yes. She's at the hospital on the island."

"Is she--is she--" He doesn't finish his sentence.

"She's alive. Stephen's with her," I answer truthfully. Keegan wipes a tear.

I move back to Murphy's side. He has an IV in his arm, and a machine beeping at his side. "I had a hard time finding a vein, but we finally got the fluids going," Sophie announces, checking her brother's vital signs.

"I'm going to take him to the hospital." I reach to pick him up.

"We've done everything we can for now. He's stable. They'll be working on Brenna, and we're almost back to the Isle. Let him stay where he is." Sophie's right, but it doesn't make it any easier to watch him suffer. I stare at the man I love. His hair's so dirty, no hint of red remains. His skin is covered in bites and bruises, and crusted sores cover his face. If it weren't for his faint energy signature, I wouldn't recognize him at all. Lacing my fingers through his, I send energy through our connection. A soft moan leaves his throat, but his eyes don't open.

"I'm here. You're safe," I whisper. "I love you."

"Highness, what was it like in there?" Tempest asks.

"Hell." No other words work as a description.

CHAPTER 4

The three-hour flight back to the castle feels like it's dragged on for days. Sophie's stopped me from jumping Murphy straight to the hospital and bypassing human transportation altogether, several times. He's stable and relaxed, and in the same condition he would be in the hospital. Her reasoning makes sense, but for the first time since discovering who I really am, I feel more elemental than human.

Seeing him like this is almost harder than not knowing. Lying on the makeshift bed Tempest made by destroying several of the plane seats, he looks so small, so fragile. I've sent a constant stream of warm energy through our touch, and his skin has slowly regained a little color through our connection.

"Ladies and gentlemen, we are approaching our destination. The current time is six forty-five in the evening, and the temperature is a balmy, sixty-four degrees. Please fasten your seatbelts, and prepare for landing." As soon as the wheels hit the runway, I jump Murphy from the plane to his parent's apartment.

Bonnie is on her feet as soon as we appear and kneels beside her son. "Oh, my gods. You found him." Tears stream down her cheeks. "Murphy, my boy." She wraps her stout arms around his shoulders, pulling him to her body. Listening to her cries tears through my soul.

"He's alive," I say, placing a hand on her arm. "Sophie started an IV on the plane. I wanted you two to see him before I take him to the hospital."

"Okay," Bonnie answers, wiping her tear-stained cheeks. "We'll meet you there."I jump Murphy to the alleyway behind the hospital. Using air, I lift his weight enough that I'm able to carry him inside without disrupting the fluid flowing into his veins.

"Help!" I call to the empty waiting room.

"What's this?" an older man asks, running to our side.

"It's Murphy McKenzie. He was held in the same place as Brenna, the woman brought in earlier, only longer." The man doesn't waste a minute. He's at Murphy's side, assessing the bites and sores in an instant.

He grabs a wheelchair, attaching the fluid bag to the hook as he rushes to the back. Within seconds, Murphy's in the same room as Brenna. "Who started the IV?" He runs his hands along the narrow tube.

"His sister," I answer. "She had a hard time."

"She did a fine job." He rubs a gloved hand over Murphy's arm. "I don't know how she found a vein. From the looks of his skin, he's severely dehydrated and malnourished. She undoubtedly saved his life."

"How is Brenna?"

He turns to the gurney behind him. "She's dehydrated and unconscious, but all of her tests have come back clear. We started an IV and preventative medicines the moment she arrived. Her heart is strong, and her lungs are clear. As far as I can tell right now, she just needs fluids and rest." He pulls a thin curtain, separating the two gurneys, closed. "Stephen donated a few pints of blood while he was here just in case it was needed."

"Dr. Rogers, is he going to be okay?" Bonnie's voice sounds weak as she and Ethan burst into the room.

"Mrs. McKenzie, that's an answer I can't give you right now. Until I have time to fully assess him, I won't know for certain." He moves back to Murphy, looking for injuries. "I don't see any immediate issues other than severe dehydration and what appears to be rodent bites covering his skin. He's stable, and honestly, that's the best we can hope for until we know the extent of the damage."

I watch as he cuts the rags Murphy's wearing off his body, revealing his sunken torso and protruding ribs. The lean muscle that once covered his abdomen is gone, replaced by something that barely looks human. Bonnie gasps at the sight. "My poor boy." She turns, wrapping her arms around Ethan's waist.

The doctor puts a hand on her shoulder. "Get some rest. We'll clean him up and make him comfortable. We'll know more in the morning."

"I don't want him to be alone. He's been alone for too long."

"I'm sorry, Mrs. McKenzie. Until we know what's going on, it's best to keep him isolated," the doctor responds. "The best thing we can do for him is give him a safe place to heal."

"I'll stay with him," I offer.

"I'm afraid that's not possible, Miss Smith. The same rules apply to all visitors. I promise to take the same care of him that I would my own son. As soon as I know something, I'll be in touch."

The three of us exit the room, leaving Murphy on the gurney, alone once more. "Adria, don't leave him. He needs a familiar face when he wakes up," Bonnie pleads, out of earshot of Dr. Rogers.

"I have no intention of leaving." Once out of sight of the glass doors, I use a combination of elements to camouflage myself into the background of the room. "I'll let you know the minute he wakes up." I watch Bonnie and Ethan walk away from the hospital. The normally jovial woman walks with a sadness that only someone on the brink of losing someone they love would recognize.

I sneak back into the room, moving far enough away from Murphy's bed, I won't be in the way. "Help me clean him up," the doctor says. I watch in silence as he and the nurse spend hours carefully cleaning and treating each rodent bite and each open wound, all while keeping a constant check on his vital signs and IV fluids. Three pans of water later, his hair has returned to its original color. Although dull and dry, the red hue shining through makes him look more like Murphy. The dirt is wiped away from his face and body, revealing bruises that were hidden underneath. With each careful wipe of a cloth and each caring caress of a hand, the two of them gain my respect.

The doctor makes good on his promise to Bonnie, and I'm grateful.

"I'll stay here tonight and keep an eye on them," Dr. Rogers announces. "Why don't you go home and get some rest? I have a few tests I want to run, and I don't feel right leaving them alone. From the looks of it, they've been through hell and back. If either of them wakes, I want someone to be here." The nurse nods, leaving the room. The doctor turns to his patients. "I don't know what you two have been through, but you've made it this far. I refuse to let you die now." He makes the last check of each one's vital signs and dims the overhead light.

Keeping myself hidden, I move to Murphy's side. "I'm here." I find myself staring at his heartbeat, flashing on the monitor behind him, daring it to drop. "I'm sorry it took me so long to find you." My words are barely audible. Lowering my ear to his chest, I listen to raspy breaths going in and out of his lungs, harmonizing with the beeping of the machines in the room. The steady beat lulls me into a trance-like sleep.

"Adria?" Murphy's deep voice resonates in my mind.

"Murphy? Where are you?"

"Adria?" he repeats. His voice sounding weaker.

"I'm here, can you hear me?"

"I can hear you." Emotion sounds through his words. *"I'm sorry I let this happen. I should've been stronger. I should've been able to fight them off."*

"This isn't your fault. Don't blame yourself. I'm sorry it took me so long to find you."

"I don't know where I am," he answers.

"What do you mean?"

"I remember rats, huge rats, and writing on a wall."

"That's how we found you. You scratched the name of the island where they took you. Ethan and Sophie figured it out, and it led us to you." I fight the tears from sounding through my words.

"I can't get out. I can't find you," he whispers, his voice fading.

"Murphy!" I sit up, finding him in the same position as before. His eyes are closed, and he's hooked to the same machines as earlier. "Murphy?" I gently shake his shoulder. He doesn't move.

"Miss Smith?" the doctor asks, walking into the room. "What are you doing here?" I released the elemental disguise without realizing it. "How did you get back here without me seeing you?"

I stand, moving away from Murphy, and wipe a tear. "I just came in. I guess we missed each other. I wanted to tell him good night. I'm leaving now."

"Thank you. Please tell your friends there's no point in them sleeping in the lobby chairs." I wrinkle my forehead in confusion, stepping out of the room as he holds the door open. "I promise to be in touch with the family if there are any changes." I nod, heading to the lobby.

To my surprise, the lobby has turned into a temporary homeless shelter. Chairs that normally line the walls are pushed together, forming beds in the middle of the room. Tempest, Keegan, and Sophie are lined up, side by side, and sound asleep. I don't wake them as the doctor suggested, instead, I pull a few of the remaining chairs from the wall and set up my sleeping spot next to Sophie's.

I wake to the sound of heavy keys rattling against the

metal and glass doors. It takes a minute to remember I'm in the lobby of the small island hospital. The two chairs I turned into a bed last night have separated, making my back feel like a twisted pretzel. Tempest and Keegan must have given up on the chairs sometime during the night. Both are in the middle of the floor and still sleeping. Keegan has assumed the position of the little spoon for the two of them, bringing a much needed smile to my face.

"What's all this?" The nurse asks, walking into the lobby.

Sophie sits up. "Good morning, Miss Flanagan. I hope we aren't imposing. We wanted to be near Murphy and Brenna."

The nurse looks at the spectacle on the floor. "Of course, dears. Let me go check on them, and I'll let you know when it's okay to come back."

"Thank you," Sophie answers. "What's going on here?" she asks, pointing at the two giants, cuddling on the floor.

"I was here first," Tempest announces.

"How did I end up as the little spoon?" Keegan asks, standing.

"Because you're small." Tempest stretches, standing next to him.

"Dude, I'm six-foot-five. I've never been referred to as small."

"Compared to Tempest, everyone's small," I add.

Miss Flanagan comes back into the room. "Dr. Rogers said you could come back."

"All of us?" Keegan asks.

"Aye, he didn't specify a number."

"Good morning," Dr. Rogers says as we enter. "I trust you slept well in my lobby?"

Keegan steps to Brenna's side, gently caressing her cheek. "How is she?"

"Are you family?" the doctor asks.

"He's her son," I interject before Keegan says something Keeganish.

Dr. Rogers smiles. "In that case, her vitals are holding steady. Her color is beginning to return, and I expect she'll be waking soon." He pats Keegan on the shoulder, who smiles weakly. Keegan picks up Brenna's hand, cradling it to his chest.

Dr. Rogers turns to Murphy. "We've got him cleaned up and have treated his wounds. I ran a full panel of tests last night, finding nothing more than the obvious. Other than severe dehydration and slight anemia, there are no physical issues that need immediate attention. We'll keep him here a few days for observation and give his body time to heal."

Sophie moves next to her brother. "Hey, bud. You look like shit."

"That'll wake him up," Keegan teases, stepping beside her.

"Aye, I thought he might need some encouragement."

"I'll leave you with them." Dr. Rogers leaves the room.

"He looks better," Tempest says, moving closer to the bed. "His color looks more natural than yesterday."

"I think I talked to him last night."

All three of my friends stare at me blankly. "He woke up?" Sophie asks.

"Not quite." I cross my arms in front of me. "It was a dream, I think. I'm not really sure."

"What did he say?" Sophie asks with tears welling in her eyes.

"He sounded weak and confused. He said he didn't know where he was, and the last thing he remembered was the huge rats and the writing on the wall."

"That happened in Petra. Why would that be the last thing he remembers?" Keegan asks what everyone is thinking.

"I'm going to go talk to Mom and Dad. They'll want the latest update." Sophie steps away from her brother. "Call me if there's any change."

"Keegan?" a whisper sounds behind me. "Keegan?" It repeats.

"Oh, my gods. Brenna!" He moves back to her side. "You're awake?"

"Where am I?" Her voice is weak.

"You're in the hospital on the Isle of Man."

"Adria? Murphy?" she asks, trying to turn her head.

"I'm here." I step to her side. "Murphy's here too."

Brenna coughs loudly. "I'll get the doctor." Tempest steps into the hallway.

"Is he...is he alive?" she asks.

"He's alive but hasn't woken up yet," Keegan answers.

"Adria?" she reaches a hand into the air. "You have to help him."

"We are. You're both in the hospital." I take her hand into mine.

"No, *you* need to help him escape. This body is nothing more than a vessel. His soul, his essence, is somewhere else, being held by Vita and Lucian." She coughs a second, deeper cough.

"I'm going to have to ask you all to clear the room," Dr. Rogers says, coming back with Tempest. "We need to assess her now that she's awake."

"I want to stay with her." Keegan refuses to move from Brenna's bedside.

"I'm afraid that isn't possible, young man. We will continue taking good care of her, and you should be able to come back within the hour." Keegan relents and steps away.

"Adria, he's running out of time," Brenna calls as we move through the door.

CHAPTER 5

Five minutes later, the three of us climb the stairs to Ethan and Bonnie's apartment. "Is there more news on Murphy?" Bonnie asks, opening the door before we get to the top.

"Nothing more than what Sophie knows," I answer. "Brenna's awake."

"Brenna?" Sophie repeats from behind her mother. "Was she able to speak?"

"She said Murphy's body is here, but his mind...his soul is still being held by Lucian and Vita."

"Is that possible?" Bonnie asks.

I sigh before answering. "One thing we've learned through all this is that anything is possible. It certainly sounds like something the two of them could and would do."

Sophie sniffs. "That means he's still locked inside her hell."

"How are we going to get him out?" Keegan moves to Sophie's side, offering comfort.

"Brenna said he was running out of time," Tempest interjects.

"Then we don't have any time to waste," Keegan retorts. "We just have to find him."

"Adria talked to him last night," Sophie tells her mother. Her voice sounds sad.

Bonnie moves to my side. "Adria? Did you talk to him? Maybe Brenna is wrong, and he's not separated?" She puts her hand on my shoulder.

I don't know how to answer without upsetting her more. "I'm not sure if I really spoke to him or if I was dreaming." Bonnie sits down heavily.

"What did he say?" she whispers. "In your dream, what did he say?"

"He told me he didn't know where he was." I try not to match the sadness in her voice.

Bonnie, the matriarch of the family, puts her head in her hands and weeps. "My poor boy. He's lost, and I can't help him." Sophie sits on the other side of her mother, pulling her close. Watching the two of them lost in their emotions brings mine to the surface.

"Ethan? Have you come across anything in your books that would give a clue to where Vita could be holding his soul?"

Ethan, normally clean-shaven and perfectly dressed, has several days of growth on his chin and is wearing clothes covered in wrinkles and stains. He runs a hand through his hair, mimicking a movement I've seen his son perform many times before. He sighs. "I've read so much over the past few days, it's all starting to run together." He moves toward his bookshelf. "I remember reading something about different planes of existence." He searches through several books, finally settling on an older leather-bound manuscript and flipping through the pages. "Here," he points to a passage. "The ethereal rest on the seventh plane, while humankind rests on the third."

"The ethereal?" Sophie asks.

"This book discusses the different planes or levels of life. Some places in the book they're called realms, other planes. However, each means the same thing. According to this, each level exists on its own, without intermixing with the others." Exhausted, he sits on the window seat. "Ethereal means light and refers to what I believe is another name for Vita."

"Is that where he is? The ethereal plane? Vita's plane?" Keegan asks.

"That would be my first guess," Ethan answers.

"This doesn't answer anything." Sophie stands, crossing her arms across her chest. "How the hell are we supposed to get to him if he's in an entirely different realm, or whatever the hell it is?"

"*We* can't, but Adria can," Tempest says, moving closer to the window.

"Wait." I wave my arms in front of my face. "We don't even know if what I heard is real. Me talking to Murphy last night could be the product of exhaustion and an overactive imagination. You all are sending me on a search party, and we're not even sure where to start searching."

"You're thinking like a human," Tempest says, reminding me of Shu.

"And, you're thinking like an elemental," I retort.

"With all due respect, Your Highness, it won't hurt to try."

He's right. It won't hurt to try, and if Brenna is right, we're running out of time. "Okay," I answer. "How do I find this 'ethereal plane?'" I hold up quotation fingers.

"That's a question for Shu," Keegan answers, looking around. "Where the hell is he, anyway?"

"He hasn't returned." I don't elaborate.

"That's helpful," Keegan answers sarcastically. "When we need him, he's nowhere to be found."

"When you talked to Murphy in the hospital, did you notice anything other than his voice? Were there any sounds? Any smells? Anything out of the ordinary? No matter how small it feels, it can be helpful," Sophie asks, changing the subject.

I think back. "It was silent except for the hospital equipment."

"What kind of equipment?"

"The machines that are hooked to his vitals. They beeped with his heartbeat."

"That's it," she answers, moving to the bookshelf. Every eye in the room is on her as she finds a colorful book, opening it to a page toward the back.

"What are you thinking?" Bonnie asks.

"I think she was hypnotized by the rhythmic beeps of the machines." She skims her finger along a few paragraphs.

"Hypnotized?" I question.

"Aye, and I think I can recreate it." She moves across the room to an old piano metronome and slides the control on the bar down, setting it into motion. The clicking keeps a steady beat as I watch it sway side to side. "According to this book, sixty beats per minute is the optimum tempo for hypnosis."

"Sophie, nothing personal, but you expect me to be able to be hypnotized with everyone staring at me?"

"Can you try?" Bonnie asks.

I sigh. "Yes, ma'am."

"Sit here." Bonnie moves from a particularly soft-looking chair in the corner. "Do you need a blanket?"

The chair feels even softer than it looks as I slide into its grip. "No, thank you. I'm not cold."

"Of course." She closes the blinds around the room, making the room resemble nighttime more than midmorning.

"Close your eyes," Sophie instructs. "I'm going to put the metronome next to your head." I nod.

"Is it possible to not have everyone stare at me?" In unison, the crowd turns their heads, finding something to stare at on the other side of the room. "I guess that works. Thanks." I slide back, stretch my legs in front of me, and close my eyes. Pulling on memories of learning how to meditate as a kid, I breathe in through my nose and out through my mouth, focusing on relaxing my body one section at a time. The steady beat next to my ear begins to crescendo through my ears and head, pounding its steady beat into my subconscious. I continue breathing, trying to focus on pulling myself to Murphy, wherever he is. Before long, the only sound I hear is the pulsating beat of the metronome, relaxing me, and calling me into its web of tranquility.

"Adria?" his voice calls.

"I'm here."

"I don't know where here is," he answers. Like before, he sounds weak and confused.

"Can you look around? What do you see?"

He pauses. *"I'm in a room. It's dark...too dark to see anything."*

"What about the smell? Do you smell anything?"

"No."

"Can you feel anything?"

"It's cold. So cold." His teeth chatter with his words. *"I'm sorry,"* he repeats his words from earlier.

"Don't apologize. I'm going to find you, Murphy. Can you move?" I ask.

"Yes."

"Tell me what the ground feels like when you touch it."

He's quiet for a while. *"Stone."*

"What is the texture of the stone? Old or new?"

"Old." I focus all of my power on sending Murphy strength and discernment. I feel the moment it ripples from my body, hopefully making its way to the intended target. *"Oh, my gods. I can feel you."* His voice sounds stronger. *"Whatever you did, I felt it."* I focus again, repeating the move. *"It feels like you're surrounding me. I feel stronger."* Tears fall immediately at his admission. *"Gods, it smells like shit in here."* I hear him grunt. *"I think I found a door, but it's sealed."*

"Look for something that will help me find you," I repeat. Several minutes pass without him speaking. *"Murphy? Are you okay?"* He doesn't answer. *"Murphy?"*

I open my eyes to five pairs of eyes staring at me. "I talked to him," I announce.

"Is he okay?" Bonnie asks. Her voice breaks with her words.

"I don't know. At first, he was confused. I sent him energy through our bond, and it seemed to help a little. He said the room he's in is made out of stone, and he found a door, but it was sealed." I fight the urge to punch something. I've never felt so helpless in my life. I hold more power than any creature on earth, yet I can't find the man I love.

"How can we help him?" Keegan asks.

"I don't know, but I'm going to do a little research. Keegan, will you come with me to the castle?"

"Of course." He opens the front door without hesitation. Out of human eyesight, I jump both of us to the castle. "Why are we here?" he asks, standing in the foyer of the grand castle.

"I want to do a little research of my own. Can you use those doctoral degrees you hold and do some online research into the ethereal realm? Maybe the internet will hold information not found in Ethan's books."

He nods. "I'm on it."

Opening the door to my room, the comfort of home hits me like a blast of cool air. I quickly change into my Phoenix gear and move to my favorite spot overlooking the water. "Air, je t'appelle à moi," I repeat the words Shu taught me during the battle with Astrid. The sky turns black on cue as dozens of air elementals answer my call. "Where's your god?" I ask the sky.

"We don't know, Mistress," the sky hisses back.

"Take me to his island." I remember Murphy telling me he had an island similar to Llyr's off the coast of France. Without an energy signature to follow, I have no idea where it is.

"Yes, Mistress." The sky responds. In an instant, I'm lifted from the balcony and moving quickly through the darkened sky, carried by the wind. Minutes later, my feet are lowered to a grassy field, and the darkness lifts.

"Where am I?"

"Île de Keller," a hiss responds as it disappears above me. The field is empty, except for an ancient dwelling that from this distance resembles a small castle. Cobalt blue skies greet me, and tall rock formations surround the crystal blue sea. I walk toward the only visible structure on the island. Is this where Shu lives? I expected something more...extravagant.

A bright red door welcomes my approach. The top of it is curved, reminding me of a cottage door from a fairy tale. "What do you want?" a voice calls from inside. "I have a gun, and I'm not afraid to use it." I feel for the energy of the person inside, finding what surprisingly feels human.

"I'm not here to harm you. I'm looking for someone. I was told he lived on this island, and since this is the only structure, I thought maybe this was his home." I fight the awkward laugh that begs to follow my words. "I'm looking for Shu."

"Who are you?"

"My name is Adria Kane, and Shu is my..." The door opens before I finish my sentence.

A man stands in the rounded doorway. He's dressed in

jeans and a button-down flannel shirt. He looks to be around fifty years old, with a head full of salt-and-pepper gray hair and a scruffy beard. "Did you say your name was Adria?"

"Yes." I smile.

"Oh, my gods. Please, come in." He sets the gun by the door. "I'm sorry about the whole gun thing." He checks behind me, looking for other visitors. "You don't get too many visitors out here."

"I'm sorry, but how do you know my name?"

"Your grandfather told me," he answers with a smile.

"How...how do you know Shu?"

"Well, that's a complicated story. Please come in. I'm sure you're able to tell I won't harm you. Hell, I couldn't even if I wanted to."

"Do you know *what* I am?"

"Have a seat." He motions to an overstuffed chair against an archaic stone wall. "Would you care for some coffee or tea?"

"No, thank you." The inside of the house is nothing like the outside. A roaring fireplace provides heat throughout the large space, and modern tapestries hang along each wall, helping to hold the heat inside. I pick up a photograph from the table beside my chair. In the picture, Shu is standing next to the human man, his arm wrapped around his waist. "Is this you?"

"Hmm?" He smiles, taking the picture. "Oh, yes. This was last year. Right before he met you for the first time." He sets the picture back in its home.

"Forgive me if this sounds rude, but who are you?"

"I'm sorry." He wipes his hand on his jeans, holding it out to shake my hand. "I'm Tucker."

"You're American?"

He smiles. "Born and bred."

"And human?"

He swipes his hands down his torso. "I think so." His smile is warm and welcoming.

"You never told me how you know Shu?"

"Oh, goodness, I didn't, did I? It's not every day I meet my step-granddaughter. I guess I'm a little flustered. Shu and I are married," he answers with a smile. "Going on twenty years now."

I'm at a complete loss for words. Shu is married to an American human named Tucker. After all the bullshit he's given me about humans, he's married to one. "That was kind of heavy information for me to just blurt out, wasn't it?" He cringes. "I'm sure there's some brandy around here somewhere if you'd prefer something a little stronger." Tucker jumps up, moving to a bar on the back wall of the room.

"No, thank you. I'm not thirsty." I pick up a second picture from the table. A small, wooden frame holds an old black and white photo. The woman in the picture looks to be in her early twenties with light hair and eyes. Small freckles line the tops of her cheeks and nose.

"Beautiful, wasn't she?" Tucker asks, sitting beside me. "Her name was Elizabeth. She's your grandmother." I study her cheekbones and eyebrows, they're the same as mine. "You look like her."

"What happened to her?"

"That's not my story to tell," he answers, patting his

legs. "Not that I'm not excited to have you visit, but I know you're not here to meet me. Has something happened to Shu?"

I set the picture back on the table. "No, he's alive. I can feel his energy, but I can't trace it. I don't know where he is. I was hoping he might be here and somehow hiding his energy signature from me."

Tucker sighs. "I don't know where he is either. He stopped by a few days ago to tell me he'd be gone for a while."

"Did he say why?"

"No, he usually doesn't. After twenty years, I've learned Shu will tell me what I need to know. I don't question him." He laughs. "It's why we've lasted this long. Of course, that doesn't keep me from being a little nosey." He smirks. "I do have my suspicions, though. I think he went after Vita."

"Vita?" I raise an eyebrow.

"You know, that bitch of an ex he has." He nods at the picture of Elizabeth. "Liz was a sweetheart. Vita, she was a psychopath."

"For Shu not telling you much, you seem to know more than the average human."

Tucker crosses his legs. "Shu tells me enough. The rest I'm able to piece together." He looks down. "There's not much more to do out here, all alone."

"I'm sorry." I don't know why I feel the need to apologize for my grandfather and his asshole ways.

"No, ma'am, don't apologize. I can leave anytime I want. I'm not helpless, nor am I a captive." He looks around the quaint room. "I choose to be here. Not only because I love Shu, but because it gives me peace. With the number of enemies Shu has, it's safer that people don't know about me, and I'm okay with being his dirty little secret."

"Do you know where he went to find her, to find Vita?"

Tucker sighs. "No, I don't. I'm sorry. I wish I did."

I stand. "I'm afraid I can't stay and visit. It's been a pleasure to meet you, Tucker."

"You, as well." He stands next to me. "I'd love for you to come and visit when you can stay longer. Bring that man of yours. Murphy? Isn't that his name?"

"Shu told you about Murphy?"

Tucker smiles. "He's told me a lot about you. You're the best thing that's happened to him in a few millennia, and he loves you dearly. He's not always the best at showing it, but trust me when I say, he loves you."

Tears fill my eyes. Shu's an asshole. He's given me nothing but shit about being human, yet he's hidden Tucker, his human husband, for over twenty years. Hearing that Shu talks about me and shared how much he loves me with someone else, melts a little of the anger away. "Thank you, Tucker. It's been a pleasure to meet you. I'll visit again."

"I hope you do!" he says as I jump back to the Isle of Man and onto my balcony.

CHAPTER 6

*B*ack on the balcony, I sit, staring over the sea. Discovering Shu's married, to a human no less, is not where I expected that trip to take me. I agree with Tucker about his whereabouts. I felt the moment Shu left he was searching for Vita, and there was definitely more to their relationship than he shared. Dammit, Shu. Why does everything have to be so difficult with you?

If Ethan's right and Murphy is trapped in some alternate realm or dimension, or whatever the hell they're called, with Vita and Lucian, I don't know how to get to him. Gods, I miss Llyr. He would know what to do.

"Adria?" Keegan calls, opening the door to my room. I wipe tears stains from my cheeks.

"Out here. Did you find anything?"

"I didn't have much time to search but found a few things on the dark web. None of it was new information. I plan to do more research later." Keegan stumbles over his words.

"Did something happen?" I ask.

"Brenna's awake again. Dr. Rogers called. I couldn't focus much after hearing that. I'm sorry." He moves to my side, and I jump us both back to the alley behind the hospital. We don't waste a minute heading through the doors and into their shared room.

"Good, you're both here," Dr. Rogers greets us as we enter. "Brenna's awake and seems more coherent than earlier." He turns toward Murphy. "He's not awake, but his color's improved, and his heart rate has slowed within normal parameters." Lacing my fingers through Murphy's, I send energy through our touch.

"Keegan, Adria?" Brenna's voice is stronger than before.

"We're here," Keegan answers, moving to her side.

"I'll give you three a moment," Dr. Rogers excuses himself from the room. Brenna turns her head, watching him leave.

"Are we alone?" she asks.

"Yes." Keegan nods.

"Adria?" I move to the other side of her bed.

"I'm here." I take her other hand in mine.

"Did you find him?"

"No, but I was able to talk to him."

"Good. If you can talk to him, you can find him." She coughs.

"Where is he?"

She takes a deep breath before answering. "He's not in this realm." Her words are getting softer. Keegan looks at me as she speaks. "When you talk to him, you're crossing to a different realm." Brenna's eyes close.

"How do I get to the realm where he is?" I ask, as her grip on my hand weakens.

"Move!" Dr. Rogers shouts, running into the room. The monitor on the wall behind her begins sounding alarms. "She's in V-fib." He pulls a crash cart next to her bed. Keegan and I step away, as he and Nurse Flanagan begin working on Brenna just like I've seen in movies and television. We watch in horror as paddles are placed on her chest, and her body convulses from the bed.

Keegan rocks from side to side, watching the woman who raised him, shocked before his eyes. I wrap my arm around his waist, offering comfort. The alarm stops as her heart rate returns to a normal rhythm. "Heart rate is steady, and her blood pressure is rising," Nurse Flanagan announces.

"What does that mean?" Keegan asks.

"It means she is one tough lady," Dr. Rogers answers. "She's stable, for now. I'm afraid visiting hours are over for the day. They both need to rest."

"What caused that?" Keegan wipes a tear as he speaks.

"I'm not sure at the moment. She was stable and much improved before you came in. It could be any number of things. I'll run a few tests, and we'll keep an eye on her." He pushes the cart back into its home. "Get some rest. I'll let you know the moment anything changes."

Knowing Murphy's body is an empty shell makes it easier to leave him there. "Come on, Keegan. They'll take care of her." I pull his elbow, directing him toward the door.

"This sucks!" he yells, kicking the brick wall once

we're out of the hospital and into the privacy of the alley. "With a capital S!"

"Yes, it does, my friend. She's in good hands, and he's right, she's one tough lady."

He leans against the wall. "I'm not ready to lose her."

"Brenna's strong. You heard the doctor. You're not going to lose her." I glance at the apartment above the bookstore. "Are Tempest and Sophie still at it up there?"

He pulls out his phone. "I'll find out." Seconds later his phone buzzes. "They are. Sophie says Rhys is awake. Maybe he'll know something."

"Has he said anything?" I ask the moment we enter. I feel like I'm grasping for straws, trying to find any new information.

"Not really. He's asked about Brenna," Sophie answers. "I didn't know what to tell him."

"Tell him the truth." I lead the four of us into Murphy's old bedroom. Rhys is sitting up, leaning against the headboard.

"Your Highness," he says. His voice sounds weak and raspy.

"How are you?" I sit in a chair next to the bed.

"I've been better." He smiles, wincing at the movement. "My back is better and finally healing. Thank you for bringing me here." He looks around the room at all of us. "Did you find Brenna?"

Keegan steps closer. "We did. She's in the hospital with Murphy." Rhys wrinkles his forehead. "Is she okay?"

"The doctor says her vital signs are improving, and her blood pressure is steady," I repeat the information Dr. Rogers told us before we left.

"I need to see her." Rhys moves to stand.

"She needs to rest." I interrupt his movement. "I think it might do you good to rest, too." Rhys concedes, sliding back into the bed.

"Rhys, we have reason to believe that Vita has Murphy, and we think her son is the one who injured you."

"Vita, has a son?"

"Lucian. And he's a giant ass," Keegan adds.

"Did he take Brenna?"

"Our theory is that she followed him." I move closer to the edge of the mattress. "Which means she's the only one who knows how to find Murphy."

"I thought you said he's in the hospital with Brenna." Rhys looks at each face staring back at him, hoping for answers.

"His body is, but his soul isn't. We think Vita and Lucian are holding his soul in another realm."

Rhys flops back on the pillow, wincing. "Holy shit." He sighs. "How the hell did Brenna follow them?"

"We found her when we found Murphy's body. We're still searching for his soul," I answer. "I don't know how she made it that far."

"The library at Castle Grimsgil," Rhys says.

"What about it?"

"There are ageless books, full of information on what you're talking about." His eyes look tired.

"Astrid's castle?" I confirm.

"They originally belonged to her mother, but yes, the same castle. There is a library in the basement where Brigit stored scrolls and books from millennia ago."

"Would these books have information on the realms?" Tempest asks.

"I don't know, but if that information is contained anywhere on earth, that's where it would be." His voice sounds weaker than before. "I'm sorry. I'm having trouble staying awake."

I touch his arm. "Thank you, Rhys. Get some rest. You've been more than helpful." On command, his eyes close as he falls back to sleep instantly.

"Sophie?"

"On it," she answers, pulling her phone from her pocket.

"Tell Daniel we need to leave now."

"Can't you just jump us all there?" Keegan asks.

"Not with humans," I answer. "Ethan?" I call, moving to the large bookshelf in the living room.

"Aye?" He closes a book.

"Want to go to a library that contains information that has never been seen by human eyes?"

"Is that a real question?" he asks with a smile. "When do we leave?"

"What about Murphy?" Bonnie asks. "What if he wakes up?"

"Mrs. McKenzie, Murphy isn't going to wake up unless we can find his soul and free it from Vita." Bonnie nods at Keegan's words, wiping tears from her cheeks.

"If there's a chance I can help save our son, I'm going." Ethan wraps his arm around Bonnie's shoulders. "Stay here, keep in touch with Dr. Rogers. I'll let you know the moment we find anything."

"Aye," she answers.

"Daniel says he can have the plane ready in twenty minutes," Sophie announces.

I turn to my security chief. "Keegan, I understand if you want to stay here, with Brenna."

He sighs. "Brenna would have my hide if I stayed here when I could help. You're right, she's one tough lady, and I have no doubt she'll be here when we get back."

I turn to Murphy's family. "We'll meet you at the airport." I jump Tempest and Keegan back to the castle foyer. "Meet back here, and we'll go straight to the airport." Both run up the stairs. "Bring weapons," I yell after them. We cleared Grimsgil when we left, but I have no idea what may have moved in since.

Upstairs, I fill a backpack with the warmest clothes I can fit inside, grabbing a pair of fleece boots and my favorite fuzzy pajamas. I fight the tears at the memory of Murphy luring me from the bathtub after Llyr's death with the same pajamas that are in my hands. Those are emotions I don't have time to feel.

Tempest and Keegan are waiting for me in the foyer, wearing fighting gear and each carrying a bag. I jump the three of us straight to the tarmac where Sophie and Ethan are waiting. Sophie assumes her job as a flight attendant as we board the jet, spreading throughout the cabin.

"This is beautiful," Ethan says, running his fingers along the plush leather seats. "It's the first time I've flown." He sits in a set of empty seats close to the back.

"You're in luck, Dad," Sophie says with a smile. "Daniel's one of the best pilots there is."

"Ladies and gentlemen, please secure all loose items, and fasten your seatbelts. We've been cleared for takeoff and will depart momentarily." Within seconds, the jet begins to taxi and is in the air. "The CAA has permitted us to push the jet to the top of our speed limitations. We will arrive in Iceland in three hours."

"Daniel's a badass," Keegan says as we continue to climb. He takes advantage of the time and sleeps on the way, while Ethan steadily takes notes and reads through a small stack of books he brought with him.

"What do you expect to find when we get there?" Tempest asks.

"To be honest, I don't know."

"Adria, can you tell me more about this library?" Ethan stops writing long enough to ask.

"All Rhys said was that it was full of scrolls and books from the last millennia."

Ethan sets his pen down. "Millennia?" The smile covering his face is one I haven't seen since this all began. I nod, happy to fuel his joy.

"We are approaching Castle Grimsgil," Daniel says over the loudspeaker. "Although the runway is longer than our last trip, this one will most likely be covered in ice. Please secure any loose items before touchdown. I'll be taking off as soon as everyone has departed in order to keep ice from forming on the wings."

"This sounds like fun," Keegan says. The plane begins to slow as we drop lower in the sky. "I don't see anything that resembles a runway," Keegan says, looking out the window. He's right. From my viewpoint, there's nothing visible except ice.

"Dad, fasten your seatbelt," Sophie demands from across the aisle. Ethan puts his papers down and quickly follows instructions just as the back wheels make contact and begin to spin the instant they hit the ice.

The front of the plane lowers, and the jet drifts side to side as it continues to roll. "Is it always like this?" Ethan asks. His knuckles are turning white as he grips the armrests.

The jet begins to slow, breaking through the ice below. "We're slowing down," Tempest announces. Slowly, the jet comes to a stop, and a collective sigh can be heard throughout the cabin.

"Compared to our last landing, that wasn't too bad," Keegan says, standing.

"Ladies and gentlemen, please gather your belongings and disembark the jet. I will be taking off in two minutes." We do as Daniel suggests, gathering our bags and hurrying down the inflatable slide Sophie released for us.

Daniel doesn't wait for the slide to deflate. The jet starts moving the moment we're down. He's turned around, heading back the way we came. "I don't think he's going to make it," Keegan says, watching Daniel fight the already frozen wing flaps. With nothing more than a thought, I push energy into the back of the jet, melting the ice on contact. At the same time, the jet lifts off the ground and climbs into the sky. "Did you do that?" Keegan asks.

"You were right. He wasn't going to make it." I turn, trying to get an idea of how close we are to the castle. All that I see are mountains and ice. "Anyone know which way the castle is?"

"I'll find out," Tempest says, changing into elemental form in front of us. Instead of the wave of water I've seen him form into several times before, he turns into a single snowflake, no bigger than a dime. He moves in front of Keegan, hitting him several times on the face before lifting into the sky and joining a few million others.

"That was something I've never seen before," Sophie says with a shiver. Keegan steps behind her, wrapping a coat around her shoulders.

"Me either," I admit. "It was cool, though." Seconds later, a snowflake lands on my hand, sliding from side to side. "Tempest?" I whisper. I watch as the snowflake raises back in the air and floats to the ice below, transitioning into a yellow-haired, green-eyed giant.

"Your Highness," Tempest says with a smile. "Castle Grimsgil is just over that crest." He points to the small snowcapped peak in front of us. "Even though it's smaller, I'm not sure that Sophie and Ethan will be able to make the climb."

"I'll carry Sophie," Keegan offers.

"Like hell, you will. I can walk it." I watch as she shivers uncontrollably in the cold.

"I have a better idea." I step away from the group, focusing my energy on the ground below. Instantly, the ice melts, revealing ancient rock beneath our feet. Air forms into tall walls, lining the path of melted snow and forming a covered path.

"That's better. Thank you." Sophie wraps her arms around Ethan and the two of them follow the newly formed trail leading to Grimsgil and hopefully answers.

The instant the castle comes into view, memories of Llyr's death and the battle with Astrid flash to my mind. The gate looks just as it did when we left with my father's body in tow. Tempest pushes the heavy gate open, revealing an empty courtyard. "Do you feel anything?" he asks.

I stretch my energy throughout the entire castle. Every tunnel, every corner, every small detail, finding nothing. "It's empty."

"This is a castle?" Sophie asks, looking around the abandoned ruins. "Looks more like a haunted house."

"I think those two words are interchangeable," Keegan answers, leading us up the ancient stone stairwell. The heavy door creaks open. With a snap of my fingers, I light a row of torches bringing the room to life.

"This is remarkable," Ethan says, rubbing his hands along the walls.

"Keegan? Can you light the fireplaces? Let's get some heat going in this place."

"Sure thing." I hear the echoes of popping fires throughout the main floor, as he uses his hybrid power to warm the frozen castle.

"Can we find the library?" Ethan asks.

"Dad, it's getting late and will be dark soon. That might be a project for tomorrow," Sophie answers Ethan's question.

"I think you're right." One look at my watch, and I realize how late it actually is. "Why don't we all sleep in one room? I don't feel comfortable separating from each other."

"I think that's for the best," Keegan agrees. "There's a room in the back with several large couches and chairs. It has a door that locks from the inside. That might be our best bet."

"Lead the way, little man," Tempest says, moving behind Keegan.

"This way, my giant friend," Keegan retorts. I'm grateful for the attempt to lighten the mood. Keegan was right. This room is perfect. It looks newer than the front of the castle, with a large roaring fireplace filling the entire wall. A heavy table sits in the middle of the room, and thick carpets line the walls and floors.

"This room gives me serious Elvis' vibes," Keegan announces, making Ethan laugh for the first time today.

"Dad and I will sleep here." Sophie motions toward an overstuffed couch against the back wall. Keegan claims a chair not far from the couch, and Tempest claims a twin to it on the other side of the room. I set my backpack on the only remaining piece of furniture. A large, antique chair, resembling a throne. Knowing Brigit, it probably is.

"Tomorrow, we'll find the library and hopefully some clues on how to find Murphy," I announce, curling on my bed for the night.

"Good night, John Boy," Keegan says with a yawn.

"What?" Tempest asks.

"It's a TV show. You can't tell me you've never seen *The Waltons*?"

"I've never seen *The Waltons*," Tempest answers.

"Seriously dude. We're having a television and movie night when this is all over. Brenna used to make me watch it every night." The room goes quiet.

CHAPTER 7

My eyes open to a strange room. Warm bedding cocoons me inside, wrapping me in comfort. "You're awake," a familiar voice says from the foot of the bed.

"Shu? What's going on?"

He's wearing solid white skinny jeans and a white sequin sweater. "I thought you could tell me. You brought me here."

I look around the opulent room. I'm lying on top of a four-poster bed. Navy blue velvet curtains line the sides of the canopy and are pulled open. Dark blue and gold leaf wallpaper covers each of the four walls, giving the room a comfortable feel. "Is this real?"

"If you're asking if I'm really here, the answer is no." He looks around the lavishly decorated bedroom. "The décor in your dreams leaves a little to be desired. It's a little gaudy, don't you think?" He moves toward a heavy wardrobe on the other side of the room. "This thing screams black plague."

"Are you really Shu?"

He moves back toward the bed. "Are you really Adria?"

I sigh, crossing my arms. "You're certainly an asshole, like Shu." I slide out of the covers, moving in front of my grandfather. "What was my grandmother's name?"

"What?" He stares at me blankly. "Why would you ask me something like that?"

"Answer the question. What was her name?"

He turns, walking in the opposite direction. "You're wasting Murphy's time, Adria. Are you sure you want to waste what precious time he has left, asking me pointless questions?"

"Yes. What was her name?"

"Hell, I don't remember. Humans all look alike. She was just a one-night fling." I think back to the picture sitting on the table at Shu's island home. Tucker told me her name was Elizabeth, and from what I gathered, she meant a lot to him.

"Leave me alone, Vita."

Shu turns, and his face takes on a strange shape. "That's absurd. Why would Vita stalk you in your dreams?" Shu knows about Hannah. He would never ask that question. I don't hesitate. I send a blast of pure energy straight into my grandfather's doppelganger. He flies backward, hitting the heavy wardrobe and breaking the door off the hinge.

"Go to hell, bitch."

Shu transforms into the familiar woman who forced

me to watch my mother drown. Vita stands in front of me. "What a pity. You ruined my fun. Why did you call me here?"

"I didn't call you anywhere."

Vita yawns. "You're boring me. Look around. Does this look like any place I would visit you?"

"I don't know what that means, and I don't care. Where's Shu?"

She smiles, moving closer. "Now, why do you think I would know where Shu is? I thought you'd be more concerned with that hunky redhead."

I send a blast of energy straight toward her, this time she dodges it, and the energy dissipates into nothing.

"Oh, look. You missed." I form the energy again, ready to strike her dead. "It's not going to work." Her voice sounds bored.

"I threw you into the cabinet moments ago. I've read that your memory is the first thing to go with age. Looks like you're having some issues."

"Your energy worked because I allowed it to work. This is my world, my realm, and I'm in control. Not some wannabe goddess."

"Where's Murphy?"

Vita laughs. "Now you're concerned about him? Took you long enough."

"Go to hell."

"You already said that. Your vocabulary is—lacking. You need a few more meaningless threats to throw my way. That one is getting old." Vita sends a blast of energy into me, throwing me out of her world and straight back to Grimsgil.

I sit up with a startle, looking around the room for anything familiar.

"I didn't mean to wake you," Ethan says, shoving papers in his backpack. "I'm just excited at the thought of what we might find in that library."

My heart is still racing from the encounter with Vita. I have no idea how she got in my head, but she did. I glance at my watch. It's still early, but Ethan's right, we need to get moving.

"You didn't wake me. It's time to get up anyway," I answer, sliding out from under the fuzzy blanket I managed to shove in my backpack. I push thoughts of Vita to the back of my mind and focus on finding the library full of hidden secrets. Somehow, Keegan's chair is moved closer to Sophie's side of the couch. They're both still asleep, and Tempest's chair is empty.

"I found the kitchen," he announces, coming back into the room. He's carrying a few unopened packages of Pop-Tarts in his hands. "There wasn't much food since lessers lived here, but I found these." He hands Ethan and Sophie each a package.

"Oh, my gods. Thank you. I'm starving." Sophie accepts the Pop-Tarts.

"Was there anything else in there?" Keegan asks.

"Not much. A couple of packs of crackers that look like they went out of date a few years ago and these," Tempest answers.

Sophie hands Keegan one of the cold Pop-Tarts. "Are you sure?" he asks.

"Aye. I have some snacks in my bag." She winks.

"That's what I'm talking about."

"Tempest? Did you see any evidence of anyone being here since we left?"

"No. I didn't look around too much, just checked the rooms closest to this room and the kitchen area. They were clear."

"Should we split up or search for the library together?" Ethan asks.

"I think together is better. Rhys said the library was in the basement. I'm guessing the best place to start would be the stairs." We head to the main staircase, finding they only go upward, and there's no evidence of any going down.

"Maybe there's an entrance in the kitchen?" Sophie suggests. We follow Tempest to the ancient room. This is the first time I've ventured into this room, and the lack of any modern conveniences is shocking.

A fireplace covers an entire wall with an opening large enough for all of us to walk inside, together. In the middle of the room sits a long table, showing years of use. Deep cuts and indentions cover the top. Against the wall, opposite the fireplace, is an ancient dry sink.

"Is this the kitchen or a medieval torture chamber?" Keegan runs his hands along the wooden table. "I can't believe you actually found any kind of food in here."

"Look around for a door," Ethan focuses our attention back on why we're here.

"I don't see anything," Sophie answers. "I even searched the corners of the fireplace. There's nothing here. The entrance must be in another room."

"If Brigit hid an ancient library full of secret information, she wouldn't make the entrance easy to find."

Thinking back on the fire castle and its hidden wings. "Maybe the entrance is upstairs."

"Why would the entrance to the basement be on the second floor?" Keegan asks a very good question.

"Because Brigit," Tempest answers. The five of us climb the ornate wooden stairs, each stair creaking underneath our footsteps. Grimsgil rivals Llyr's castle in age, but where his has been modernized over the years, Grimsgil is trapped in a one-thousand-year-old time warp. The heavy stairs are worn from use, many of them missing large chunks of wood from centuries of use. The halls split at the top of the stairs, heading in opposite directions. Ancient torches line the walls, and Keegan beats me to lighting them, filling the hall with dancing shadows of light.

"This place is so dark and dreary," Sophie says.

"Aye. Keeping the rooms dark and curtains closed helped keep the heat from escaping into the cold outside," Ethan answers. A series of doors line the hallway. Most are standing open or unlocked, holding large wooden beds that match the décor of the rest of the castle.

Keegan stops in front of one of the many doors. "This was my room." His voice is soft and full of emotion.

Our group looks into the small room. The only furniture is a now broken bed and a wooden chair. "This looks dreadful," Sophie announces.

"It was," he scoffs and laughs awkwardly. He shivers, shaking off a haunting memory, and we continue moving down the hallway.

"This one's locked," Ethan announces, standing at the last door in the hall.

"Does it have a keyhole?"

"Aye, looks like a skeleton key." He runs his hands along an old metal locking mechanism.

"That key could be anywhere. Let's try the other side before we tear up every room looking for the key." We follow Tempest to the other side of the castle, finding every door standing open and no hidden entrances to the library evident in any of them.

"Do we have to use a key?" Keegan asks. "Can't you use your powers and open it?"

I shrug. "I can try." There are moments when I forget I hold the power of four elements, then there are moments I forget I'm human. Walking back to the door, I feel for any energy that might be hiding and feel nothing. Using a combination of air and earth, I picture the lock releasing and the door unlocking. Just as I imagined, the lock pops, and I open the door to a bedroom that rivals the rest of the castle. Thick red carpet pads the floor as we enter. Modern, decorative wallpaper covers all four walls, leading to a modern bathroom. A large tufted velvet headboard sits between a king-size bed and the far wall.

"What the hell?" Keegan says, taking the words out of everyone's mouths. "Did we just time travel?"

"No, but it sure feels like it. Why is this room straight out of *Better Homes and Gardens* and the rest of the castle is from a game of *Dungeon and Dragons*?" Sophie runs her hands along the raised velvet wallpaper.

"This must've been Brigit's room." Tempest stands in the doorframe. "It makes sense that she would make her lessers live a thousand years in the past while she lived in the lap of luxury."

"Look for a hidden door that could lead to the library." For the next few minutes, we tear the room apart, inspect every inch of the walls, and search behind every piece of furniture, finding nothing.

Sophie plops down on the mattress that's now on the floor. "Where would she hide it?"

"Brigit was crazy, but she was smart. If she had information she didn't want to be discovered, the entrance would be somewhere no one could find easily," Ethan says, walking across the large expanse of floor. As he walks, the boards creak under his steps. As he moves closer to the fireplace, the creaks change pitch.

"Ethan, stop." I move closer to him, stepping on the same board he is. It responds to my weight, rewarding me with a soft moan. "Go back where you were, and walk this way again." Ethan doesn't question me and retraces his steps. The change in pitch is even more obvious this time. "Does anyone else hear that?"

"Aye, it sounds different," Ethan answers.

Tempest and Keegan don't hesitate. Finding the corner of the carpet, they pull the edge until the carpet gives way, revealing thick hardwood floors hidden underneath. They continue tugging the carpet and its underpadding loose until they reach the spot where we're standing, revealing what looks like hinges and a small cutout of the wood. "Is that a door?" Ethan asks.

Tempest kicks at the wood, trying to loosen it from the rest of the flooring. "It's not budging."

"Step back," I warn the group around me. Combining air and earth, I become one with the ancient birch used to form the floor, releasing the seal that's been in place for centuries. The door opens followed by a release of air and dampness. Tempest pulls the door open completely, revealing a pitch-black hole.

"Is this it?" Ethan asks.

"It's something." Keegan grabs a lighted torch from the hallway. "I'm going first."

"*We're* going first," Tempest interrupts. "We don't know what's down there. You might need help."

"You first, big guy." Keegan nods, handing him the torch.

"Be careful. Tempest's right. We don't know what's down there." I watch the two of them descend what looks like a winding staircase.

"Please be cautious with that torch. If this is the entrance to a priceless library, we can't take the chance of damaging any manuscripts." Ethan shifts nervously from foot to foot. We watch until they disappear into the blackness. The faint hint of light continues, but the two of them are no longer in view.

"What do you see?" Sophie yells into the hole, getting no response. Moments later the room fully illuminates, sending light to the entrance. "Dad, you have to see this." Ethan moves closer to the hole. Inside, a crystal chandelier hangs just beyond the metal staircase, casting a glow on what looks like rows and rows of bookshelves, each filled to the brim with books and scrolls.

"Oh, my gods," Ethan whispers.

"It's clear," Keegan calls up the stairs.

"After you," I motion for Ethan to lead the way. His eyes are as large as saucers, and a look of childlike wonder covers his face. The room is larger than I expected. Several small lights are scattered over the walls, providing more light the lower we go. How she has electricity in this room is beyond me. A tall rolling ladder leans against every wall, allowing readers to reach the top of each shelf.

"This is unbelievable." Ethan wipes a tear. "The amount of lost information that could be found in this room is unfathomable." A fire roars to life as Keegan finds a fireplace in the corner. The heat fills the room, taking the goosebumps with it. "I don't know where to start," Ethan admits. "This amount of information could take years to consume."

"We don't have years," I remind him.

"Aye, my son's life depends on what we find in here. That fact hasn't eluded me."

"The last time I visited a library, there was an old-fashioned card catalog. You don't think she'd be that organized, do you?" Keegan looks through several drawers in the bottoms of the bookshelves.

"If this library is true to its time, there will be nothing like that. Texts were organized by continents in older libraries," Ethan answers.

"So, there'd be a section for each continent?" Keegan clarifies.

"Possibly." Ethan walks to one of the walls, pulling out a large text. "This book is written in Sanskrit."

"So, that section is from Asia?" Sophie crosses her arms across her chest, taking in the massive size of the bookshelf.

"Yes, however, the one next to it is written in what looks to be an ancient form of Swahili." He scratches his head. "That rules out continents. Most libraries from this time period were religious. I'm at a loss as to how this one is organized."

"This was Brigit's library. She was the goddess of fire. Is it possibly organized by element?" Tempest's voice bounces off the walls of the small room.

"That's genius," Ethan says, opening the ancient book again. "This book is about the element of air." He opens the one next to it. "So is this one." He looks up with a smile. "I think you're right!" Pointing to the wall opposite, "Sophie, check those books."

She follows directions, opening a small, leather-bound book. "I don't know this language."

"Try another one."

"It's Gaelic," she announces, flipping through a second book. "It seems to be talking about water." She picks up another one, copying the movement. "So is this one."

"How many languages do you read and speak?" Keegan stares at his crush with newfound respect.

"Fluently, around thirty. Not nearly as many as Dad," she answers.

We all stop, staring at Ethan. "What?" he says with a shrug. "Last count, I was fluent at around one hundred and twenty, but I recognize bits and pieces from around twenty more."

"So, if you all are right, this wall," I motion to the books behind Ethan, "is air. And this wall," I motion toward Sophie, "is water. That means the two remaining walls are earth and fire. That leaves one problem. Where's the information on aether?"

"It would be much smaller," Ethan answers. "In all my

years I've only seen brief mentions of it scattered through a handful of books."

"I'm thinking Brigit would keep it somewhere very secure," Keegan says, gently pulling books from the shelves.

"I don't think we're going to find it in books. That information would be older, ancient. Look for a set of scrolls, possibly hidden or inside of something larger." Ethan moves toward a dimly lit corner. "Somewhere like this." He moves a heavy vase from the corner. "Look inside dark containers, anything unusual."

We scatter throughout the small room, each carefully moving priceless pottery, and thick texts, and looking for anything that fits Ethan's description. "Dad!" Sophie exclaims. She's moved to the center of the room, to a large wooden table, and gently unrolling something that looks like paper.

"Stop!" he warns. "That's papyrus. Don't try to unroll it until it warms up." She moves it closer to the fireplace, setting it several feet from the flames.

"Here's another one," Keegan says, placing it next to the other.

"Is this one?" Tempest stands, holding a third roll of ancient paper.

"Possibly. Bring it with the others." Ethan's in his element, and I smirk at the comparison.

"Here's another," Sophie says, bringing it to the group. "I don't see anymore."

"We have to let the scrolls sit in the heat until they are completely warmed up. If we try to open them, the papyrus will crumble in our hands. It may take a few hours or even a few days."

"Do we have a few days?" Sophie asks.

"Truthfully, I don't know. Brenna said he didn't have much time left," I answer.

"We can't rush these texts. They could hold the answer to saving Murphy along with the answers to the universe." Ethan walks to the opposite wall. "Saving my son is my first priority, but if we destroy the information that could save him, we might as well be condemning him to death ourselves." Sophie moves beside him, putting her arm around his waist.

"Then we'll wait," I answer. "In the meantime, I'm going back to the hospital to check on Murphy's vessel and Brenna. I'll grab some food while I'm there. You three will need to eat."

"Thank you," Keegan says. "If Brenna's awake, tell her I love her." At that moment, I see something in Sophie I haven't seen before. Her eyes soften when she looks at Keegan. Hearing him profess love for the woman that raised him just gained him major bonus points.

"I will." I smile. "Any requests for food?"

"This is soup weather," he answers. "Can you transport soup through a time warp or whatever it is you jump through?" There go his bonus points.

I laugh for the first time in days. "I'll try." I disappear, leaving my friends in an ancient library, deep in the mountains of Iceland, and jumping into the hidden alleyway next to the hospital on the Isle of Man.

CHAPTER 8

"Perfect timing," Dr. Rogers says as I walk through the front doors of the hospital. "I was just about to call you. Mrs. McKenzie is already in Murphy's room."

"What's going on?" My anxiety is reaching an all-time high.

He waves his hands in front of him. "He's fine. In fact, he's much improved today."

I sigh internally. "Can I see him?"

"Of course, follow me." He leads me into their shared room.

"Adria?" Bonnie says, leaving Murphy's side. "How are you here?" She looks behind me for more members of our entourage.

"I just flew in." She nods in understanding.

"I think he's on the uphill swing. His vitals have been steady for the past twelve hours, and his breathing is back to normal. He's gained five pounds with the fluids we've been pushing through his system."

I suddenly realize Murphy's bed is in the room alone. "Where's Brenna?"

"She's been moved. We felt it was better to separate the two of them. She seemed slightly agitated when they were together." Agitated? His reasoning seems strange, but I don't question it.

"Can we have time alone with Murphy?" Bonnie asks, sharing a sweet, motherly smile with Dr. Rogers.

"Yes, ma'am. Let me know if you have any other questions." The moment the door swings shut, "Have you found anything?"

"We found the library and what we think are ancient scrolls that hopefully will hold the answers we need." I keep my voice low. Bonnie wraps her arms around my waist. "Oh, Adria. I can't thank you enough."

"Don't thank me. Ethan and Sophie are the ones doing all the work. He's brilliant."

Bonnie laughs. "A regular genius, he is. Can't match a pair of socks to save his life, but he can spend an hour telling you pointless information."

"With any luck, we should know something within the next few days. Ethan's afraid the scrolls are going to fall apart when opened, so they put them in front of the fire to warm up." She nods. "How's Rhys?" I ask.

"He's much better today. In the next day or so, he should be well enough to visit Brenna." I walk closer to Murphy's vessel.

"He feels so...empty."

"Aye, I agree." She rubs his arm. "At least his body is healing."

"I'm going to try to visit him again when I get back to Iceland. Last time it seemed to help." She wraps her arm around my waist for the second time. "He's lucky to have you."

I gently run my fingers through an escaped curl. "I think I'm the lucky one."

Bonnie pats me on the shoulder. "Don't make me cry."

Dr. Rogers walks through the swinging door, followed by Nurse Flannagan. "I'm going to have to ask you to leave. We want to hold any external stimulation down for a while."

"Can I visit Brenna before leaving?"

"She's asleep. I just left her room."

What happened to Dr. Rogers? He's acting strangely. I search his energy, finding nothing that wasn't there before. "Okay. Can you give her a message for me when she wakes up?"

"Of course." He smiles a smile that doesn't reach his eyes.

"Tell her Keegan says he loves her."

"I'll make sure she gets the message." He opens the door for our exit. "I'll be in touch if anything should change." We walk out of the hospital and toward the apartment together.

"Was he acting differently to you?"

"Aye. I've known John for thirty years. That wasn't him." I stop walking.

"What do you mean?"

"I don't know how to explain it. He felt...different."
Holy shit, a human picked up a change in energy, and I
didn't.

"Bonnie, I want you to go straight to the castle. I'm
going to get Rhys, and we'll meet you there."

She wrinkles her forehead. "I need to get a few things
first."

"No, I want you to go straight there. I can't jump you
there since you're human. I'll call Stephen to meet you
halfway. Don't stop at your home, and don't talk to
anyone."

"Adria?"

"Please, go now." She turns without questioning me
and walks as fast as she can toward the fountain. I send a
text to Stephen, who responds immediately. I run to the
upstairs apartment and Rhys's bedside.

"Adria?" he questions. I hold a finger to my lips. He
nods. Laying my hand on his shoulder, I take us to the
castle and Llyr's office. "What's going on?" he asks,
looking around.

"I don't trust anyone right now." Glancing out the
window, I see the front end of the black SUV crossing
over the ancient mote. Gods, I need to give Stephen a
raise. He parks by the front doors, and Bonnie runs inside.

"What's going on?" she asks. "What's with all the
cloak and dagger?"

Before answering, I focus on a ball of energy,
combining all four elements into one and placing a protective barrier around the entire perimeter of the castle and
grounds. Stephen locks the heavy wooden doors behind
him. "Thank you, Stephen."

"My pleasure." He walks throughout the bottom floor, closing all the drapes, and hiding us from the world outside.

Bonnie crosses her arms in front of her chest in protest. "Adria, I have a roast in the oven."

"I'll get it." I motion to a chair next to the couch Rhys is occupying. She sits unhappily. "I'm sorry to be so secretive, but you were right. Dr. Roger's energy was off. I believe he's been taken over by another entity."

"What?" she lowers her arms and relaxes her stance. "What are you saying?"

"You said the Dr. Rogers we talked to wasn't him."

"I meant that figuratively," she mocks.

"You may have, but I think you're right."

"You think Lucian took over John Roger's body?" Stephen asks.

"I do."

"Oh, my gods. Murphy?" Bonnie jumps to her feet, pacing in front of the fireplace.

"I don't think he'll harm him. They have his mind. I'm certain they let us take his body. The rescue was too easy." Bonnie sits dramatically at my words.

"What about Brenna?" Rhys asks. He sits up, sliding to the back of the couch.

"I don't know. Dr. Rogers said they separated her from Murphy and wouldn't let us see her."

Rhys struggles to stand. "That's a bunch of bullshit. Excuse my language, Your Highness. We have to get to her." He winces with pain. "He'll make sure she's dead this time. He won't let her live. If she's gone..." He doesn't finish his sentence.

"I'll go. I've placed a protective barrier around the castle grounds. You're safe here." He nods, and I help him sit before jumping back to the alleyway behind the hospital. I call on the power of air, blending into the elements surrounding me and hiding my energy signature within them. I feel around for Brenna's energy, feeling nothing. Shit. I send energy throughout the buildings, searching for any familiar elemental energy on the island. Something deep below grabs my attention. I focus on it, letting it pull me toward it, and jump straight to the source, finding myself in the ancient catacombs deep below the city. Like before, I blend into the floors and walls, hiding my energy as I move. Brenna's energy grows stronger the further I move.

"Adria?" a voice echoes through my mind.

"Brenna?" I respond the same way.

"He's here. Lucian's here."

"I know. Where are you?"

"Hiding. I'm in a dark room. I don't have the energy left to jump." Her voice sounds weak.

"Open your energy to me. I can't find you." Instantly, her power surges through the tunnels, and I jump straight to it. Brenna's tiny body is slumped in the back corner of one of the rooms underneath the hospital.

"Brenna!" I shout, moving to her side. "How'd you get down here?"

"You're not the only one who can get where she wants, quickly. This is as far as I made it. I don't have any strength left." Moving to her side, I put my hand on her shoulder, taking us straight to the castle and setting her on the chair next to Rhys.

"Brenna?" Rhys grunts, trying to sit up. "Where was she? Is she...?"

"I'm alive," she whispers. "Just out of juice. I need to refuel, and I'll be fine."

"I found her in the catacombs."

"How the hell did she get there?" he asks.

"Apparently, like Firsts, Brenna has the power to jump through energy and travel anywhere she wants." I look at the elderly woman, wondering what other secrets she's hiding.

"She needs to rest. I'm going to take her upstairs." Stephen cradles her to his chest and leaves the room.

"Thank you." Rhys follows them with his eyes. "I need to be with her," he moans.

"She's going to be fine. Her energy is already regenerating. You need your rest."

"Could that bastard have been draining her energy? Is that why it's taken her so long to heal?" Bonnie asks a question I haven't thought of.

"It would make sense. That would explain why her heart stopped when she was talking to me and Keegan."

"Why would he do that?"

"Because that's what they do," Rhys answers. "It's why Lucian comes in people's dreams. Emotions feed energy. Stronger emotions provide more energy. Scaring the shit out of someone in their sleep produces higher levels."

I move closer to the couch. "You're saying Lucian gains strength through scaring humans, and then stealing the energy that produces? That's why he compared himself to a vampire."

"That's exactly what he is, an energy vampire," Rhys confirms.

"She's resting comfortably." Stephen comes back into the room.

"Good. Thank you, Stephen. Can you contact Daniel and find out how quickly he can get the jet back in the sky?"

"Of course." He exits the office.

"What are you thinking?" Bonnie asks.

"I'm thinking I need to get you and Stephen the hell off this island."

"I can't leave." She protests. "Who's going to man the store while Ethan's gone? He'll have my head if I close the doors."

"Something tells me he'd rather have you alive than keep the store open." Bonnie steps back with a surprised look. "I'm sorry to sound harsh, but Lucian's here, and he's not here for teatime. I can get Brenna and Rhys to Iceland with me, but you and Stephen can't travel the same way. You have to go by plane." Bonnie relents, nodding her head. "No one is safe here."

"What about Murphy? I know that's just his body, but I can't leave him here." Tears well in her eyes.

"I don't have any intentions of leaving his vessel. Once I know you are in the air safely, I'll get him there too. I promise." She nods, wiping the tears from her cheeks.

"Daniel said the jet will be ready in a half hour," Stephen announces.

"Good. Pack a bag. You and Bonnie are heading to Iceland."

Stephen looks confused. "It's not a request. Bonnie

will fill you in on the way to the airport." He nods, heading into a back room while I jump to Ethan and Bonnie's apartment. Grabbing a bag from her closet, I fill it with a combination of clothes, undergarments, and heavy sweaters. Something's better than nothing. Making a quick trip through the apartment, I turn off the oven and turn on a few lights.

I jump back to the castle and hand her the bag. "Goodness, girl. Did you pack my clothes?"

"I tried." I smile. "I hope there's something in there you can wear."

Stephen comes back into the office. "Daniel called. He said we can be off the ground in five minutes."

"Good. Leave the SUV on the tarmac, we'll worry about it another day." He nods. "Lucian got through the island wards. It'll only be a matter of time before he's through the castle ones as well. I'm going to follow you to the airport and make sure the jet is safely off the ground before we go." I follow them through the door to the garage. To my dismay, there are no supercars. Just twin SUVs. When this whole thing is over, I'm buying a bright red Ferrari. I've never been the "legal" owner of one before, just one that I "borrowed" as a kid.

The three of us climb into the SUV, and I make myself invisible, blending into the elements and hiding my energy signature. He hits the gas and is away from the castle within seconds.

The airport is less than a mile ahead, and Daniel has the *Smith Industries* jet waiting in its usual place. Stephen and Daniel both need raises. Like we'd practiced it a hundred times, Stephen screeches to a stop beside the jet as he and Bonnie run straight to the awaiting staircase. I stay hidden as the stairs rise and the jet begins to taxi. Something feels off the minute they begin moving.

I jump into the cockpit assuming the position of the copilot beside Daniel, who stares straight ahead and is not wearing headphones. "Daniel? Is everything okay?" He doesn't respond and continues to stare ahead, blankly.

Ahead of the jet, the runway is growing shorter, and from the looks of it, Daniel has no intentions of pulling up into the sky. I focus all four elements into a strong blast of energy, sending it through Daniel, and into the thing that has control of him from the inside. Like a scene from a horror movie, Lucian, or what looks more like the ghost of Lucian flies out of Daniel's body, through the side of the plane, and out of the cockpit. "Pull up!" I scream, exiting the jet and following Lucian. I watch as the jet rises in the sky, barely missing the end of the runway and the sea beyond. Lucian is near the castle. I feel him. That bastard's trying to get into my home, into Llyr's home.

I jump straight to his energy. He feels me the instant I arrive and turns into a solid form right in the middle of the village, in front of humans. Shit.

"Hello, Adria." His singsong voice is sickly sweet. "I thought I'd pay a visit to your castle. Although, I'm quite impressed with the protections you have around it."

I don't respond. Instead, I circle to the other side of him, focusing on keeping my energy disguised. He doesn't turn to follow, which confirms my suspicion that he doesn't see me, just feels me. I send my energy to the fountain, making the water reach over twenty feet into the sky.

"There you are." He moves toward the fountain. I do

it again, this time sending my energy toward the beach. I watch as his signature follows the source. Getting him away from the castle, I jump into Murphy's room at the hospital and to his bedside. Nurse Flannagan is standing next to his bed and drops the chart she's holding the moment I appear.

"Miss Smith? I...I didn't see you come in." She laughs awkwardly, looking around the room for answers.

"I'm sorry. Sometimes, I'm quieter than I intend. Guess it's my military background. Where's Dr. Rogers?"

"He stepped out for a moment. Can I help you with anything?"

"Actually, yes. I'm thirsty. I'd love a glass of water." I smile my best smile.

"Of course," she says, picking the chart up off the floor. "Let me get a few more readings on him before I go."

I cough loudly. "I need it now if you don't mind." I grab my throat, being as dramatic as possible.

"Sure. I'll be right back." She smiles, no doubt thinking how helpless I am.

I wait until the doors close behind her before placing my hands on Murphy's shoulder and jumping us to the castle. I gently lay him on the floor of the office, next to the couch where Rhys is laying. "Is that Murphy?" he asks.

"What's left of him. I'm going to get Brenna, and the three of us are going to Iceland."

"Can you carry three people with you?" he asks.

"We'll know soon." I find Brenna in one of the guest rooms.

"Adria," she says with a smile. "I'm feeling stronger already."

"Good, I'm going to need your help to get us out of here." I help her sit up. "Bonnie, Stephen, and Daniel are on their way to Iceland. We're going to go our way." She nods, understanding.

"I'll do what I can."

"Can you stand?" I pull her to her feet. She nods, wobbling slightly when I let go. "I'm taking us downstairs." We jump to where Rhys and Murphy are waiting.

"Brenna!" Rhys struggles to stand. She shuffles to his side.

"Well, aren't we a crew?" Brenna says, a smile sounding through her voice. "You're going to take all three of us, plus yourself, to Iceland?"

"That's the plan."

"We need to move close together." Brenna sits on the edge of Rhys's couch. He wraps his arm around her waist. I pull Murphy close to her feet and cradle his head in my lap. Brenna and Rhys each put a hand on my shoulders, and I focus all my energy on getting the four of us to safety.

"Brenna?" Instantly, I feel an extra shot of energy as she shares enough power to boost our transport out of Llyr's castle, sending us to Brigit's. I open my eyes to the newly decorated office and push thoughts of Shu from my mind.

CHAPTER 9

Three hours later, I've rearranged the furniture in the office and have Rhys, Brenna, and Murphy placed on makeshift beds scattered throughout the room. A local fire lesser that Rhys reassured me was trustworthy has agreed to pick the humans up at the airport when they land. Rummaging through the kitchen, I've managed to find enough ingredients to make something similar to the vegetable soup Keegan requested. When I left Grimsgil, I had no idea I'd be gone this long. No doubt their Pop-Tarts and snacks have long since worn off.

Goose bumps cover my arms and legs in an instant. I drop the bag of food, not sure what, if anything, is about to happen. Small pricks of energy bang on my shield, begging to be let in. Something's trying to get through the barrier I wrapped around the castle. Stepping outside, I pull my energy signature inside myself, hiding me from anything not human. Headlights from the black SUV come into the courtyard. As soon as it stops, Bonnie, Stephen, and Daniel exit. Thank gods.

"Adria!" Bonnie says, moving quickly up the stairs.

"You made it." I wrap my arms around her shoulders.

"Barely," Daniel answers. "What happened back there? I blacked out, and when I woke up, we were almost at the end of the runway."

I smile. "You had an unwanted guest."

"I'm not sure what that means, but thank you."

"How's Murphy?" Bonnie asks.

"He's good. Through Brenna's recommendations, I brought a human nurse from the village to watch them all. She's been here for around an hour. She's got Murphy hooked back up to an IV, and Brenna is up, moving around."

I lead her into the room they're sharing. "Mrs. McKenzie," Rhys says. "I owe you my life."

"Oh, pishposh." She gently touches his shoulder on her way to Murphy's bedside. "You healed yourself. We just needed to get you to a safe place." She gently rubs Murphy's cheek. "I'm here, my sweet boy. Come back to us."

The nurse walks into the room on cue. "Bonnie, this is Mary. She's our nurse." Mary nods her head with a smile.

"Pleased to meet you, Mary. Thank you for your help."

"My pleasure, ma'am." I pull the three of them out of earshot of Mary.

"Bonnie, I need to go to Grimsgil. They're bound to be hungry, and the scrolls should be warm enough to open without damage. Will you be alright if I go?"

"Yes, dear. We'll be fine."

I look at Stephen and Daniel. "I've strengthened the protection wards around the castle. You will be safe here." I move even closer. "Mary doesn't need to leave this castle until I get back. She's the most susceptible to Lucian away from the safety of the wards." Both men look back into the room.

"Understood," Stephen answers.

Back in the office, I move to Brenna's side. "Mary, please excuse us for a minute." I wait for her to leave the room before asking the question I've been dying to know. "How did you know where to find Murphy?"

Brenna turns to face me. "I followed a trail of bread crumbs that led me straight into a damn trap."

"Why didn't you come to me for help?"

"There wasn't time."

"I need you to tell me everything you know. Tell me about the realms."

Brenna sighs before answering. "Millennia ago, when I was still with Brigit, she talked about the realms and Vita's control over them. I didn't pay attention to Brigit's ramblings at the time, but when I found Murphy in Greece, I knew his soul was nearly gone, and it all made sense. I knew without a doubt that Vita had transported that part of him to her realm."

"None of this makes sense. Why did Lucian come here? He had to have known I wasn't here. What was the point?"

"I wouldn't pretend to know what goes on in his mind. However, everything about your life has been planned from the beginning by that bitch. I have no doubt that my following Lucian to Murphy wasn't part of the plan." She takes my hand into hers.

"How do I get there, to her realm?"

"I don't know. But if you've found her library, you'll find the answer." She sits up. "It's something only you can do. No one else will survive jumping into her realm. The answers are in the library." She looks toward Murphy's shell. "He's running out of time. Without his soul, this body will begin to deteriorate and eventually die."

Rummaging through the kitchen, I discover a few storage containers perfect for transporting soup. Let's hope it *is* possible to transport liquid. Remembering the medieval kitchen at Grimsgil, I grab bowls, spoons, and plates. "I'll stay in touch," I say to the room before jumping back to Grimsgil with soup intact.

"Adria?" Keegan says as I stand in the middle of the ancient kitchen. He gasps when he sees what's in my hands. "You brought food!"

"I did." I set it on the long table. "Where is everyone?"

"Sophie and Ethan are in the library. I was looking for food...and look, I found some." He picks up the containers of soup.

"Where's Tempest?"

"I'm here, Your Highness. I was walking the perimeter and checking the rooms."

"Good, I'll let Ethan and Sophie know there's food." I jump to the basement library to find them sitting on the floor in front of an ancient scroll.

"Adria!" Sophie smiles.

"You two look like you've found something."

"We're having a little trouble translating it, but it's

definitely something about Vita." Ethan grunts as he stands.

"Why don't you take a break? I've brought food."

"We're on the verge of discovery. I can feel it," Ethan answers. "I need to stay down here."

"You need to eat," I remind him. "Thirty minutes isn't going to change anything. Murphy's safe and here in Iceland." He looks up.

"Did something happen? Why is he in Iceland?" Sophie asks.

"It's a long story. We'll discuss it while you eat." The two of them reluctantly follow me up the winding staircase and to the kitchen.

Sophie's stomach growls loudly. "Whatever you brought smells wonderful. How long have we been down there?" she asks.

"I've been gone at least twelve hours."

"No wonder my eyes are crossed." Sophie rubs her eyes dramatically. We enter the kitchen to find the ancient table set for a meal. Keegan is carefully pouring soup into three bowls and setting the table for five.

"Dinner is served," he says, using a voice straight from a cartoon.

"Gods, you're weird." Sophie laughs.

"I know. It's part of my charm."

"Why did you bring Murphy's vessel to Iceland?" Ethan asks, taking a sip of his soup.

Tempest looks up in question. "Murphy's here, in Iceland?"

"So are Rhys, Brenna, Bonnie, Stephen, and Daniel."

"Did you bring a bus?" Keegan stops eating.

"Something like that." I recall the events of the day, making sure to include every minor detail. Like children at story time, they hang on every word. I end with the delivery of the soup.

"Makes my day sound boring," Keegan says, pouring himself a second bowl.

"How close are you to translating the scroll?" Sophie and Ethan share a look.

"I think we're close. It's not written in any language I recognize, but the symbols are familiar." Ethan moves away from his soup. "I need to get back to work."

"Aye. I'll be there in a moment." Sophie takes another bite.

"Is he alright?" I ask, watching Ethan leave the room. He's moving slower than I've seen before, and he has a slight limp with his walk.

"Aye, just tired and worried." Sophie stands, picking up the empty bowls on the table.

"I think we all are." Tempest stands. "I feel helpless just sitting around this empty dungeon of a castle."

"Why don't we go on patrol?" Keegan suggests, cleaning up the rest of the leftovers. "We can explore the barren ice fields. It'll give me a chance to practice burning things."

"That does sound thrilling," Tempest answers. Hearing him use sarcasm surprises me. He's never sounded more human. Being that it's at least thirty degrees in the castle, I don't worry about keeping the leftovers cold. The entire castle is one huge refrigerator.

"Is Mom okay?" Sophie asks as we climb the stairs back to the library room.

"I think so. She's worried about Murphy, but she's strong and determined. If you're worried about them being alone at the fire castle, Brenna's with them, and her strength is returning quickly. They'll be safe for a little while. The castle is heavily warded." We enter the posh room where the entrance to the library was hidden.

"Find anything?" Sophie calls down the hole.

"Come down. I need your eyes." We slowly descend the ancient metal staircase to find Ethan sitting in front of a large scroll, writing in a notebook.

"What's this symbol look like to you?" He points to what looks like scribbles left by a kindergarten student.

Sophie studies the spot for a while. "A raven maybe? Either that or a... a phoenix?"

"Adria? What do you think?" Ethan asks. "What do you see in this image?" I move to the scroll, studying the intricately drawn ink spot. The creature has a long flowing tail with long wings and what looks like fire around the outside.

"I see a phoenix," I answer, no louder than a whisper.

Ethan runs his hands through his hair, making it stick up on the end. He walks around in a circle. "That's what I saw too."

"What does that mean?" Sophie asks.

"I don't know." He carefully rolls the scroll back to its original structure. "I've never seen reference to a phoenix in any of the writings before."

I scoff. "That's a little ironic."

"What do you mean?" he asks.

"The phoenix. That's what the elemental trainers are called. I even have a picture of one on my training gear." I point to the faded image of the phoenix, leftover from before my life changed forever. "That's a strange coincidence."

"One thing I've learned through all of this is there is no such thing as a coincidence." Ethan gently carries another of the scrolls to the table. "Maybe we'll find more information in the next scroll. Let's see if this one is ready to unroll." Together, Ethan and Sophie painstakingly pull the scroll edges, opening the first section. "This one looks to be written in Sumerian."

I look between the two of them. "Is that good?"

"In a way, yes. It's a language that Dad reads, however, depending on which region this scroll is from the symbols may mean something different," Sophie answers, while Ethan pours over the images.

"It's going to take a while, but I think I can transcribe this one." Ethan slides his glasses off his head and over his eyes, studying the ancient scroll.

"Take whatever time you need. I'm going to go check on the boys." Ethan doesn't respond.

"I'll stay with him." Sophie moves to his side.

I feel for the dynamic duo's energy, surprised to find they've somehow managed to move miles away from the castle. I jump to their location to find Keegan, peering over the edge of a very familiar cliff. The beach below is where my father, Llyr, lost his life.

"What are you doing?" I question, moving behind him. He physically jumps, lightening the heaviness of the location a little.

"Gods, Adria. Don't sneak up on me like that. I could have burned you to a crisp."

I laugh out loud. "I don't think you're that strong."

"True, but I would have tried." I join him, peering over the side of the cliff.

"What are we looking at?"

"Tempest. He went down there. He's been walking around for a while. I don't know what he's doing."

Sadness fills me. "This is where Llyr died. Even though you both were at Grimsgil when it happened, maybe he can sense the significance."

"I'm sorry, Adria. I had no idea."

"It's okay. I'll go down and talk to him." Keegan nods. I ride the wind, landing on the black sand with a soft thud. "Tempest?" He's kneeling next to the water. The seven-foot giant sniffs and wipes his cheek before standing.

"Your Highness." He bows with his words. "I'm sorry. I...something called me here."

I fight the tears filling my eyes. "This is where he died." My words are no louder than a whisper. Tempest turns back to the sea.

"They told me." I've never heard him sound so sad.

I walk toward the gentle giant, wrapping my arm around his waist. "I miss him too." I lean my head on his massive arm as the two of us stare into the open sea.

"He loved you," Tempest says, wiping his cheek.

"I loved him."

"Thank you for coming down here with me." He turns back toward the cliff wall. "We better get back before Keegan decides to try to climb down. In case you haven't noticed, he's not the most graceful."

I laugh, wiping my eyes. "I noticed that within the

first five minutes of meeting him. May I?" I ask, holding my arm out to him. He lays his hand on top of mine, and I take us to the top of the cliff with a blink.

"Everything okay?" Keegan asks.

Tempest nods. "I was able to properly say goodbye. Not only was he my God, he was my friend."

I move between them, wrapping an arm through each of theirs. "We need to get back. Ethan was studying a new scroll when I left. He may have found something by now."

"Should we jump?" Keegan asks.

"I think that's a great idea." The three of us disappear from the top of the cliff.

......

Back in the library, we find Ethan looking much the same as earlier. He's hunched over an ancient scroll, writing feverishly in his notebook.

"Dad, it's well after midnight, and you need to rest." Sophie yawns, stretching her arms high above her head.

"I'm almost there, Sophie. I can feel it. You all go to sleep. I'll wake you if I find anything."

Sophie looks to me for help. "Mr. McKenzie. You're not going to do us any good without rest."

He stops, putting his pencil down. "With all due respect, Adria, I'm not going to do my son any good if I stop. I'll rest when I can't go any further."

"Then, I'm staying here with you," I answer, finding a spot on the floor to sit.

"Aye," Sophie agrees. "Me too."

"We'll stay here, too, if that's alright," Tempest says,

speaking for he and Keegan. I nod in agreement. We spread throughout the tiny library, making sure not to touch anything of value. Hell, this entire library is valuable. It doesn't take long before the only sound I hear is the scratching of Ethan's pencil on his notebook and soft snores. The rhythmic dancing of flames from the fireplace, combined with Ethan's pencil, pulls me into a meditative trance.

"Adria?" Murphy's voice whispers through my mind.

"I'm here."

"I'm tired." His voice is weaker than before. I focus on sending energy to him. *"I can feel you, but it's not helping as much this time."*

"We're close to finding you." I fight the tears from sounding through my voice. *"You have to hold on."*

"It's so cold here. I feel so weak, so helpless."

"Can you see anything?" I ask, hoping something has changed.

"No. It's dark."

"Are you alone?" He doesn't answer. *"Murphy?"*

"I think so." He sounds further away than before.

"Did you move?"

"No," his voice is barely audible. My eyes open in an instant. I jump from my vision, startling everyone awake.

"Adria? Did something happen?" Sophie asks.

"He's running out of time."

"I've got it!" Ethan yells. "It doesn't make any sense, but I've got it."

"What are you talking about, Dad?" Sophie moves to Ethan's side.

"See this symbol?" He points at the scroll. "I've been

struggling to figure out what significance it holds. Then I remembered something I read years ago about the Sumerian language. Occasionally, symbols were reversed, almost like a reverse negative from a photo. By flipping the image and rotating it 180 degrees, I was able to complete this picture." He turns his notebook to show everyone.

"It's a phoenix," Keegan announces. Sophie pulls the notebook toward her.

"Another one?" she asks. "What does this mean?"

"There are no coincidences. We've found references to a phoenix in two different scrolls from two different regions of the world who never had contact with each other," Ethan answers. "Let me translate the rest of this. It won't be as difficult."

"Phoenix?" Keegan asks. "As in a huge bird that dies by flames and rises from the ashes? Those kinds of phoenixes?"

Ethan stands up. "It's a prophecy."

"Can you read it?" Sophie asks.

"Aye, I think so." He clears his throat. "The one who is made of water and air, yet breathes fire and brimstone, holds the power to stop the rebirth of the phoenix of all."

"What the hell does that mean?" Keegan asks.

"It's about Adria," Tempest answers.

CHAPTER 10

*H*ow can an ancient prophecy, written in an archaic language be about me? "Don't take this the wrong way, but there's no way I'm the person that prophecy was written about." No one answers. "Seriously, you all don't think for one minute that it's about me." I turn to Ethan. "Does it say anything else?" He shakes his head.

"You were born of water and air and hold the power of fire and earth. There's no one else that fits into that mold," Tempest continues.

"Vita's the phoenix, and you hold the proverbial water hose," Sophie completes the thought.

I stand, walking around the small room. "You all can't be serious."

"It makes sense, Adria." Sophie moves next to me.

"No, it doesn't. It makes no sense at all." I look all of them in the eyes. "I'm a kid from California who grew up in foster homes. Prophecies aren't written about me.

That's the stuff from fantasy books and movies, not real life."

"Buckle up, buttercup. It's about you," Keegan adds his words of wisdom.

"What does that even mean?" Tempest asks.

"It's a saying." He pauses. "I really don't know what it means; it just seemed fitting."

"Well, it was weird." Tempest's reprimand makes me laugh.

I turn to Ethan. "Let's say this crazy notion is true, which it's not, and Vita is this phoenix, which that— might be true. It still doesn't tell us how to get to her realm and to Murphy."

"Not yet, but if Vita is the phoenix, I need to change what I'm looking for." He switches the scroll out for another of the rolled-up versions. "I'll keep looking." He gently rolls out the new scroll, moving in slow motion. "Get some rest, it'll take a while."

I wake later to the sounds of soft snores to find everyone, including Ethan, is asleep. With no windows in the library, I have no idea if it's noon or midnight, however, this far north in Iceland, a window wouldn't help anyway.

After Ethan's discovery earlier, I need to talk to my best friend. Murphy's the only one I can truly open up to. He's been my rock since this insanity started, and now, he's out of reach. Gods, I miss him. How selfish do I sound?

Murphy's soul isn't in our realm, but his vessel is. I jump to the fire castle and his bedside. Brenna has moved her bed closer to Rhys, and the two of them are holding hands while sleeping. I move to Murphy's side, touching his cheek.

"I don't know if you can hear me, but I need to think you can." I wipe a stray tear. "I've never felt so alone." Gods, it sounds even more selfish coming out of my mouth than it did in my head. Murphy's trapped in another realm, being held captive, and here I'm feeling sorry for myself. Staring at the shell of the man I love, I count the freckles lining his cheeks. The bruises and bites that once covered his face have mostly healed, making him appear almost normal.

"You'll be shocked to know Shu disappeared again," I whisper. "I'll have to tell you all the crazy shit that goes along with that later." I laugh, awkwardly. "Thanks to Rhys, we found an ancient library beneath Grimsgil where Brigit hid information that Ethan thinks will help find you." I sniff. "By the way, your dad's a genius. Did you know he speaks over a hundred different languages? He and Sophie are in the library now, and Ethan feels like he's on the brink of discovering something that will help us find you." I lean over, kissing his cheek. "I need you to stay strong. I'm coming. Don't give up on me."

"Adria?" Bonnie interrupts.

I sniff, standing. "It's me. I'm sorry to disturb you."

"You didn't. I was just coming down to check on everyone." She moves to the other side of Murphy. "His body is improving, for now." I nod with a sniff. "Is Ethan getting enough rest?"

"He was when I left. Although, I don't think it was intentional."

Bonnie huffs a laugh. "If I counted the number of

times that man fell asleep while he was working, it'd be in the millions. You're going to have to make him rest."

"That's easier said than done."

"You're not telling me anything I don't know." She laughs.

"What are you two talking about?" Brenna says, sliding from her bed.

"Men," I answer.

"That sounds boring." Brenna moves to my side. "I'm feeling more like myself. I can help where needed."

"Good, we're going to need everyone we can get." Placing Murphy's hand on his chest, I turn fully toward Brenna. What do you know about phoenixes and Vita?"

"Phoenixes?" Bonnie repeats.

"That's something I haven't heard for a while." Brenna moves toward the double doors that exit the room. "I don't know much, but I'll share what I do know. Let's go for a walk." I follow her through the doors, into the foyer. "I don't think I'm ready for a walk around the compound. How about we take a tour of the inside?"

I nod, following where Brenna leads. Branching off of the main hallway, she heads toward a part of the castle I haven't yet explored. When Brigit lived here, she blocked over half of the castle off for who knows what reasons. I never had time to explore and have no idea what's behind some of these doors.

Brenna looks around the hallway with a nostalgic gleam in her eyes. Centuries of dust line the baseboards and peeling wallpaper covers the walls. "This wing has been blocked off for at least a century," she says, running her fingers across intricately carved woodwork. "My room was down here." She leads us further down the hall, past paintings of people I don't recognize to a plain wooden door. "This is it." The door slowly creaks open, revealing what many historians would deem a time capsule. "This is a surprise. I figured Brigit would've burned anything that was once mine. Not much has changed."

An old wardrobe stands open, one door barely attached. Ruffled fabric and lace spill into the room. Brenna runs her fingers across one of the items, breaking off the pieces of the ancient fibers with her hand. "Gods, I hated it here." Seeing her like this feels almost intrusive. For the first time since I've known her, her guard is down, and she's allowing me to see the real her. Other than the fact that she's a badass and the first fire lesser ever created, I don't know anything about this woman who saved my life and has sworn to fight to the death to protect me.

She sits on an old settee that looks like the only weight it will withstand is dust. Surprisingly, it doesn't collapse. "This place was hell for me." She pauses, rubbing her fingers along the splintered wooden armrest. "I was nothing more than a plaything for Brigit. Something she could dress however she wanted, sell to whomever she wanted, or use for whatever pleasure or pain she felt like causing at the moment."

"Millennia had passed and other lessers were created by the time I lived in this room. Even though I was still in hell, this room was the beginning of the end." She wipes her cheek, walking toward the remnants of what was once a bed. "This is where I planned my escape." She laughs. "I knew no matter where I went, she'd look for me until she found me. I needed to hide my energy from her if I wanted to survive." She moves toward a boarded-up window.

"That's how I ended up in the village. If she found me in what was nothing more than a village of a few families, I could lie my way out of it. Finding me somewhere else would be more difficult to explain." She laughs at the memory. "I learned how to hide my energy. It took years to master, but when it finally worked, I got out. I cut my hair off, covered my skin with anything to transform it, and hid in plain sight. Hours turned into days turned into weeks turned into years and eventually centuries." Walking back to the middle of the room, she said, "You know what's funny? She came into my store once or twice with Astrid and didn't recognize me."

I've never known Brenna's story. Hearing it makes me respect her even more than I already do. "You are incredibly strong." My words are inadequate.

She huffs a laugh. "Strong is never a word I used to describe myself. Desperate, maybe? But not strong."

"Desperate people are capable of amazing things. Sometimes when we're at our worst is when we're at our best." I move in front of her and wrap my arms around her small shoulders. "I'm so glad Keegan introduced me to you. We wouldn't be where we are today without you."

Brenna returns the gesture, wrapping her frail arms around my waist. "Me too. Speaking of Keegan, how's my boy?"

"He's good. Probably on the brink of starvation, but he's been a trooper." I pull away from our embrace, giving her one last squeeze. "He sends his love."

"Gods, I love that kid." She laughs. "He thinks I saved

him. Truthfully, it's the other way around." She claps her hands, ready to change the subject. "So, phoenixes, huh?"

"Phoenixes," I confirm, leaning against the wall.

"Over the millennia, I've heard tales of creatures that live throughout many different realms. Phoenixes are just one of many." I'm dying to ask questions but stay quiet as she pauses. "They live in the same realm as Vita. What information did you find about them?"

Propping my boot on the wall behind me, I say, "Ethan found a hieroglyph of a phoenix on an ancient scroll and a prophecy that mentioned a phoenix in another."

"Prophecy?"

"That's what Ethan called it."

"Do you remember what it said?"

"Not every word." I try to remember as much as possible. "She who is born of water and air, and then something about fire and brimstone, holds the power to control the phoenix of all. That's my paraphrased version."

Brenna stares at me. "Did it use the words phoenix of all?"

"Yes. That part I remember. Tempest thinks I'm the one that the prophecy talks about." I laugh. "Isn't that absurd?"

"Maybe not."

I step away from the wall. "Brenna, you can't believe this shit too. I'm a punk kid from California, not someone prophecies are written about."

"Adria, how many people do you know who are born of water and air and also control fire and earth?"

"I don't know, maybe there's one out there."

"Now who's full of shit?" Brenna stands.

"If that prophecy is true, then you hold the power to control the phoenix."

"Not you too?" I move toward the door.

"In the seventh realm, each element is represented differently. In our realm, the gods and goddesses control each element, but the seventh is different. There, each element is represented by a specific phoenix. Not an actual phoenix, per se, but a figurative one."

I stop. "What are you talking about?"

"The seventh realm is the ethereal realm, Vita's realm."

"Have you been there?" I move away from the door and back to my position on the wall.

"No, the only information I've heard has been through word of mouth throughout the years." She sighs. "The phoenixes are not what you think they are. They're not like what we see in movies and books. They're not birds that fly and burst into flames. They're Llyr, Shu, Dagda, and Brigit, only in another realm."

I sit on the edge of an ancient chest, not caring if it breaks. "Is Llyr still...alive there?"

"His body? No. The impression of him? Yes. But it's no different from here. His impression is still alive here, through you. You are the embodiment of Llyr's spirit in that realm, just as you are here. Llyr's spirit is alive inside of you. Just as Brigit, Dagda, and even a part of Shu are as well. When you inherited their powers, whether, by blood or other means, you became them in all realms. *You* are their phoenixes."

I take a minute, allowing her words to mill around my brain. "So, there is a version of me in the seventh realm?"

"Yes."

"And this version of me is what has the power to control the 'phoenix of all,' Vita?"

"According to the prophecy Ethan found, it seems that way."

I sigh. "How the hell do I get to this part of me and get Murphy out?"

"That's above my pay grade, I'm afraid."

"Who would know?" I cross my arms in frustration.

"Why do you think Brigit built that library at Grimsgil? She spent many millennia searching for answers."

"Why haven't you told me this before?"

"I assure you I wasn't keeping it a secret. When you live as long as I have, things slip your mind after a few thousand years. It wasn't until you mentioned the phoenixes that I remembered." Brenna moves toward the door. "You don't have much time. Murphy's body may be healing for the moment, but his soul is still trapped. You need to get back to that library and fill in the blanks."

"I know." I follow her through the maze of hallways and back to the foyer. Daniel and Stephen come down the stairs at the same time, meeting us in the foyer.

"Good morning," Stephen says with a slight bow. "I'll get breakfast started."

"Good morning. Thank you, Stephen. Could you make three extra servings? I need to take some with me."

"Of course."

Back in the study, I'm surprised to see Rhys sitting on

the edge of his bed. His color almost looks normal, and he's moving freely. "Good morning, Rhys."

"Good morning, Your High...Adria."

"You look more like yourself."

"Thanks to you and Bonnie." He stands. "You saved my life."

I dismiss him with a wave of my hand. "Anyone would have done the same."

"Either way, I owe you my life." He walks toward the kitchen, moving a little slower than normal, but moving.

"Where do you think you're going?" Brenna asks.

"To help with breakfast. It's my job."

"I think you're still in need of a few days of rest," she retorts. "Stephen can handle it."

"That's *my* kitchen," Rhys argues without stopping. "I promise to sit down if I need to."

Brenna relents, letting him continue on his mission. Half an hour later, Stephen has the table set with a meal that looks fit for a king. He hands me three to-go boxes which will make one hybrid and two humans very happy. "I knew those would come in handy one day," Rhys says, coming into the dining room. "I've had those to-go boxes for years."

"Brenna, I'm going to Grimsgil. I'll let you know the minute Ethan finds anything. Hopefully, he already has." She nods.

"Highness," a deep voice booms, entering the castle.

"Tempest? What...did you swim here?"

"The sea isn't my only means of transportation." He smiles. "Ethan's found something. He insisted that I retrieve you immediately."

"Oh, goodness. It must be important. Ethan never gets in a hurry for anything," Bonnie says from the table.

"I'm ready." I wrap my arm through his, jumping the two of us, along with breakfast, back to Grimsgil.

"Perfect timing!" Ethan says as we appear in the library. "Come, come!" He stretches a scroll flat on the table. Keegan happily takes the food from my hands, murmuring a quiet thanks to whoever cooked it.

"What's this?"

"This is a different Sumerian scroll." He points to a line toward the bottom. "This one talks about the realms." He pulls his glasses from his head. "Let me read it to you." Like there's another option. "This symbol is the phoenix." He points to the now familiar picture. "We figured that out before you left. This one," he points to one on the other side. "This one represents the number seven." I nod. "This entire line combined talks about the seventh realm and how to travel there." Following the pictures, he reads his discovery. "The seventh realm is only accessible by the prophecy foretold."

"That's you. You're the prophecy foretold," Sophie fills in the blank.

"Only the prophecy can enter the seventh," Ethan continues.

"I have no idea what that means," I answer truthfully.

"Me neither," he agrees.

I move away from the scroll. "This is great and all, but it still doesn't tell me how to get to the seventh realm, or even if that's where he is." I try not to sound as frustrated as I feel.

"When Vita or Lucian appear to you, in our world,

how are they showing themselves?" Keegan sets his breakfast down and joins our conversation.

I shrug. "Vita pretended to be Hannah and gained my trust."

"What about Lucian?" he asks.

"Gods, I don't know. I think the first encounter I had with him was on the Isle when he was inside Murphy's body."

"Every time they've been in our realm, they've used someone else's vessel." Sophie moves back to the open scroll. "That's the key. You have to travel through another vessel."

"I may be the Goddess of All Elements, but you're going to have to dumb this down for me. What are you saying?"

"Murphy is your way in," Ethan whispers, looking at the scroll. "That's how you'll get there. Murphy is your portal."

"He has one foot in our realm and one foot in hers," Keegan adds. "He's the key to entering her realm."

I remember watching Lucian step into Murphy's body in the catacombs. "Could it be that simple?"

"Aye, it could be," Ethan whispers.

"Tell me what to do."

CHAPTER 11

The ground outside Grimsgil has thawed enough to allow Daniel to land the jet and keep it on the ground longer than a few minutes. After Ethan's discovery, I've jumped between the two castles several times, getting everything and everyone coordinated. The consensus was for all of us to join together at the fire castle and away from Grimsgil. Ethan's spent the past hour gathering books from each of the elements and filling his backpack to the brim, while Tempest and Keegan worked on securing Grimsgil the best they could.

"Daniel's almost here," Sophie says as Ethan climbs the staircase out of the library. "He can wait long enough for us to board, but any time after that will only make his chances of taking off less. He's managed to find a spot close to the castle this time, so we don't have to walk."

"Adria, can't I stay a bit longer? There's so much information down there. I could help so many people with the knowledge held in those books," Ethan begs.

"I'll set wards to hide and protect it the as best I can. When we get through all of this, we'll come back." I hate making promises I don't know if I can keep. Ethan nods, knowingly.

"He's landing now." Sophie rushes her father through the halls, leading them toward the awaiting jet. "Let's go," she says as the two of them run toward it. Within minutes, the jet begins to taxi down the makeshift runway and lifts high into the sky.

"Want me to follow them?" Tempest asks, coming behind me. "If they have issues, I can help."

I nod. "That's a good idea." In an instant, the seven-foot giant transforms into a snowflake no larger than my fingernail and disappears into the sky.

"I'll never get used to seeing that," Keegan says, taking the words out of my mouth. "The castle is as secure as possible. There's only so much you can do to lock a thousand-year-old building." He looks behind him. "It won't take much to get inside."

"I added some wards around the perimeter and throughout the inside to keep the library as safe as possible. There's not much more I can do." I reach my hand out. "Ready?" He nods, laying his hand on top of mine. I jump the two of us to the foyer of the fire castle.

"Keegan?" Brenna walks out of the study with her arms held in a hug position. "I've missed you, my boy." He picks her up in a bear hug.

"I was so worried about you!" his voice cracks with emotion.

"Good thing I'm hard to kill." She laughs.

Bonnie walks into the foyer, looking around for the

rest of her family. "They're on the jet, and Tempest is following behind." She nods, understanding. "They should be back in less than an hour. Any change with Murphy?" I walk past her into the study.

"His body seemed to be healing, but it's gone downhill in the past few hours. Without his soul inside..."

Brenna escapes Keegan's arms. "I don't like the thought of you doing this alone."

"Aye, me neither," Bonnie adds.

I smile, glancing between the two of them. "I'm not a fan either, but there's no other way. Ethan found more evidence. He thinks the only way to get to the seventh realm is by using Murphy as a portal."

"How do you do that?" Bonnie asks.

"I'm not sure. I witnessed Lucian do it in the catacombs, but I'm not sure of the exact science or if there is one."

"Where the hell's Shu?" Brenna asks. "He might be able to travel with you to her realm." I haven't shared information on Tucker or that Shu's possibly Lucian's father with anyone since finding out. I answer with a smile and a shrug.

Stephen joins the crowd in the study. "Daniel just called. They're doing fine and should land in the next few minutes. I've taken the liberty of checking the runway at the airport, and it's open for traffic."

"I'll go get them." Rhys limps out of the kitchen.

"Like hell, you will," Brenna takes the words out of my mouth. "You've been on your feet for the past several hours. You need to rest." Rhys frowns but doesn't argue.

"I'll go," Stephen interrupts, heading out the front door.

"Do you have a plan for when you get to Vita's realm?" Brenna holds Rhys's arm, helping him back to his bed.

"I don't know what I'm going to run into when I get there, so, no." I follow them, stopping at Murphy's bedside. His hands feel clammy, and his skin is paler than earlier. "He doesn't look good." Bonnie moves quickly to my side, assessing her son.

"Oh, Adria." Tears fill her eyes. "I don't know how to help him." Brenna makes eye contact with me. Her silence speaks volumes. There's no time left. Without his soul, Murphy's body won't make it much longer.

Brenna moves closer, dismissing the nurse from the room. "What you're going to see when you get there is nothing like here. Things won't be as they seem, and Murphy won't be himself. Trust your instincts, your power, and *nothing* else." I nod, pulling my hair high on my head.

"What can I do?" Keegan asks.

"Keep them safe," I answer, looking around the room. "You're all I have left, and I love each of you dearly. If I don't ret..."

"No, we're not going to take this conversation there," Keegan stops me. "You're going to come back, and you're going to have Murphy with you." He wraps his arms around my shoulders, pulling me tight.

"Agreed," Brenna says, reaching an arm around the two of us. "We'll be waiting, right here, when you *both* return."

Bonnie wipes a tear as she joins our group hug. "What's going on here?" Tempest says, coming through the door. We separate, laughing awkwardly.

"Just saying our goodbyes," Bonnie says.

"The humans are on their way back." The giant water elemental lowers himself to one leg. "My Queen, I would give anything to go with you and fight by your side. I would protect you with my life."

"Tempest, I have no doubt you would, and I'm eternally grateful for your desire. But this is something I must do alone."

"I understand." He stands and wipes his cheek. "Keegan and I will handle things here. Rescue Murphy. Rescue my friend."

I lay both my hands on his shoulders. "I have no doubt you and Keegan will do what needs to be done here. I trust you with my kingdom and my life." I turn to Brenna. "If I don't..." I pause, remembering Keegan's words from earlier. "Brenna, you are in charge of the fire elementals. They trust you, they'll listen to you. Get them to safety if the need should arise." She bows her head.

"Tempest, you are in charge of the water elementals. I trust you'll know what to do."

I move back to Murphy's bedside. "I'm not sure how to do this," I admit.

"Use him as your entry." Brenna moves beside me. "Think of the times you've spent together, fought together, and grown together. Harness the power from it, and use it to take you to him."

Closing my eyes, I think back to racing him through the lake at the compound, meeting and eating dinner with his family, and making love for the first time. Warmth fills every pore as the emotions of my thoughts threaten to overwhelm me. A low pulsation fills my core and quickly turns into a vibration, gaining speed as my thoughts scroll through mine and Murphy's times together. My body begins to pull toward something I have no words for. The tug starts low in my core and spreads quickly throughout my body.

I open my eyes as the familiarity of the castle disappears, turning into rocky hillsides and mountainous terrain. I'm standing on the edge of a cliff, surrounded by roaring seas and pouring rain. Is this it? Am I in the seventh realm? "Murphy!" I yell into the vast expanse. "Murphy! Where are you?"

The only sound is the crashing of the sea as it pummels the cliff below. The rain is so heavy, I can barely see two feet in front of my face as I walk in the opposite direction of the sea.

"Murphy!" I yell again, my voice cut short by the overwhelming volume of the water below. Dammit, this rain is relentless. "Etach spak dune!" I shout into the sky. Nothing happens.

I close my eyes as the rain stings my cheeks with each brutal blow. I pull my thoughts inward and picture the rain surrounding me. I imagine it stopping and allowing me to see where I'm going when it leaves.

To my surprise, when I open my eyes, the rain has done just that. I close my eyes again, this time envisioning the overcast sky and fog-covered basin. I picture the fog lifting and the sun rising high in the sky, giving me the ability to see what surrounds me. I open my eyes and am met with clear skies and open land in front of me. Holy shit, I can't believe that worked.

I spread my energy as far around me as possible. Searching for anything familiar, finding nothing but a complete lack of everything. I continue moving away from the cliff and toward the vast expanse of nothingness.

After walking along the monotonous rocky ground for what seems like hours, nothing has changed. Each rock looks identical to the one before, almost as if I'm walking in circles. This can't be right. Vita's playing some kind of game with me. Finding a smaller pebble, I make a scratch along one of the larger rocks and keep moving. Several minutes later, I walk past the same rock, finding my scratch in the same place as earlier. "Shit!" How stupid can I be? Vita has me in some sort of loop, and I've wasted hours repeating the same few steps.

I close my eyes, envisioning Murphy. *Take me to him,* whispers through my mind. When my eyes open, I'm standing on what looks like a busy city street. People are moving around, going about their lives, oblivious to the confused goddess, standing in front of them.

Growing up in Los Angeles, I'm no stranger to living in a big city. They're loud, stinky, and always busy. Wherever I am is the complete opposite. No one acknowledges anyone else. In fact, it's like they don't see anyone other than themselves. Cars are silent as they move through the congested streets. The world reminds me of a video game, and I'm surrounded by groups of "non-playable characters."

"Can anyone hear me?" I shout into the crowd. Nothing changes. I'm invisible to them.

An older man, wearing a three-piece suit, is heading straight toward me. I resist the urge to move, instead, I stick my foot out, deliberately tripping him. He falls to the ground face-first and disappears before slamming into the concrete below. What the hell? I continue walking through the silent crowd, looking for anyone or anything that might lead me to Murphy. Each person that I pass is nothing more than an empty shell. An NPC.

Out of the corner of my eye, I notice a young girl that seems to be looking at me. I turn to face her, making eye contact fully. She smiles and waves. Oh, my gods, she sees me. She slides her finger to her lips, silencing me before motioning for me to follow.

I stay several feet behind as she leads me off the main street and into an empty alley. "Hello, Adria," she says once we're alone.

"Do I know you?"

"We knew each other once."

"I'm sorry. I don't remember you," I answer truthfully.

She smiles. "You wouldn't remember me. It was a long time ago."

"What is this place?"

"This is the ethereal realm."

"Do you live here?" I place my back against the cinderblock wall, helping me feel less exposed.

"Sometimes. I come to this realm when I'm sleeping."

"You're human?"

The girl shrugs. "Of course, aren't you?" I don't answer.

"What city are we in?"

"It's Los Angeles."

"This can't be Los Angeles. I grew up there. This is nothing like I remember."

"It's where we knew each other." She smiles again. "We were in the same foster home for a few days. I shared my bed with you one night when you didn't have one."

The memory of my last foster home comes to mind and the young girls I left to fend for themselves. "Oh, my gods. You were the one that let me inside my last night?" She nods. "I've thought about you often. I'm sorry I left you there. I should've figured out a way to take you, take all of you, with me."

"No, you did the right thing. You wouldn't have been able to take care of all of us." She laughs. "If I remember right, you were barely able to take care of yourself." The truth behind her words stings. "It didn't matter anyway. They moved me, a few days after you left, to a new home."

I take in the features of the young girl. She looks the same as she did that night. "That was seven years ago. Why do you still look the same?"

"Time isn't the same here," she answers with more wisdom than I've heard from many adults. "This is where I come when I need to escape. Sometimes it looks like this, sometimes it looks like a forest, and sometimes, I imagine an ocean."

"Are your places all the same?"

"No. I visit different places." She grabs my hand, pulling me out of the alley and into the silent street. "These people can't hear you. They're just part of my dream. Or I guess, our dream."

"I'm sorry, I don't remember your name."

"Mira," she answers.

"That's right! Now I remember," I lie. "Mira, do you think you can teach me to go where I want?"

She stops walking. "Probably."

I pull her to a stop. "I've lost a friend of mine. He's trapped in this realm, and I think he's being held against his will."

She wrinkles her forehead. "That's silly. How would he get trapped? All he has to do is wake up."

I sigh before answering, not sure how to explain something I don't understand myself. "A horrible person trapped him here, in this realm. Not all of him, just his soul. Back in my realm, his body is dying without his soul inside."

Mira pauses. "Then he's probably at the castle."

"Of course, he is. Where else would he be?" I laugh. "Can you take me there?"

"Oh, you don't have to actually go there. All you have to do is imagine it, and that's where you'll end up. This is the dream world. Anything is possible."

"I can do that." I squat down to her level. "Mira, are you okay? Are you safe? If I leave you, will you be alright?"

She smiles, wrapping her arm around my waist. "I'm here all the time. It's you I'm worried about."

"No, I mean are you alright in your foster home?"

"Yes. They're nice to me. There's food to eat and a warm bed, and I even have toys." She smiles, pulling me tighter. "I'm good."

"Thank you," I hug her back. "If you ever need anything, I want you to come to this world and call me. I'll do my best to find you." She nods her head.

"All I have to do is picture the castle, huh?"

"Yep. I like to make it look like a princess castle. You can make it look like whatever you choose. That's the magic of this place. You create your own world."

"Sounds like a plan." I close my eyes and choose the place I'm most comfortable with, Llyr's castle on the Isle of Man. When I open my eyes, Mira's gone, and the familiarity of home stands in front of me.

CHAPTER 12

*E*xcept for the vintage hue overlay covering the scene in front of me, the courtyard, castle, and the surrounding seas look no different than usual. The energy is strange. The comfort this view usually brings is gone, replaced by an uneasiness that I find impossible to describe.

I send my energy throughout the castle, looking for any trace of Murphy. I feel nothing. In fact, I'm not sure my energy ever left my body. In this realm, I feel more human than elemental.

What looks like my ancestral home on the outside is anything but, on the inside. A modern home, with sheetrock walls and contemporary furnishings greets me the moment I enter. What the hell is this? This realm reminds me of a crazy dream. "Hello?" I call through the emptiness. "Is anyone here?"

An older woman scuffs her feet, as she walks across a

tile kitchen floor into the room I'm in. "Oh, hello!" She smiles weakly. "Are you hungry?"

"No, thank you. Who are you?"

"I didn't hear you come in," she continues, ignoring my question. "We don't get much company here. Please, have a seat." She motions to an empty chair at a round table.

"Are you alone?"

"Are you hungry?" the woman repeats.

"No, ma'am. Are you alright?"

"Of course, dear. Why do you ask?" She sits at a round table and takes a sip from a cup of something that looks to have been sitting there for a while.

"I just walked into your home. You're not concerned?"

"Of course not. Are you hungry?" she repeats for the third time.

I touch her shoulder, and my arm passes through the illusion in front of me. She turns her head toward me and smiles. What kind of a game is this? Was Mira even real or just another one of these non-playable characters? Nothing but a distraction, an illusion to keep me guessing.

"Vita!" I yell through the house. "I'm tired of your bullshit!" The older woman disappears instantly. I move to a window next to the table, pulling back the curtain. Outside, the familiarity of Llyr's castle is gone, replaced with dark skies and lightning flashes in the distance.

The facade of the kitchen disappears into nothing, just like the void where I've spent so much time looking for Murphy. "You've always loved being the center of attention. Why are you hiding now?" I yell into the darkness.

The black of the void transforms into ancient stone-covered walls and floors. "Vita! I don't have the time or the patience for your games." Walking through the ancient halls, I run my fingers along the illusion. The texture feels real under my touch. "Why do we have to play games? You know I'm here. This is childish."

The stone hallway seems to continue forever. Is this another loop? One I don't have time for. Mira's words about the magic of this realm come to mind. Stopping in the middle of the hall, I imagine the stone giving way to a beautiful beach from home, and in an instant, I'm met with water lapping against white sandy beaches.

"Is this a game to you?" I shout over the roar of the water. I send my energy out in all directions, searching for anything familiar. Again, I'm met with nothing. Dammit! Vita will keep me in this loop until time runs out for Murphy.

Ethan's reading of the prophecy comes to mind. "The seventh realm is only accessible by the prophecy foretold." Ethan and Sophie assumed the prophecy was written about me. What if the seventh isn't an actual figurative place, but something internal? Something that each of us holds inside. I sit on the sandy beach, overlooking the water, and breathe in the refreshing comfort of the sea. Remembering my only good foster mother and her love of meditation, I cross my legs, relax my arms, and concentrate on slow cleansing breaths.

In through my nose, and out through my mouth. "A fast breath in is like a spiritual reset," she would tell me. I do several fast breaths followed by a slow, calculated release of air. The moment the energy changes, I feel it throughout my entire body.

I open my eyes to the familiar background of the California compound. On the seawall overlooking the water sits Murphy and beside him is a very naive me. I looked pissed, while he's desperately trying to explain the craziness of the elemental world to me. I smile at the memory of this day. It was the first time Murphy tried telling me the truth of who I am. The scene switches to the hot tub on Llyr's veranda. My head is resting on Murphy's shoulder, and a smile covers his face. This was the day I learned Shu was responsible for keeping me hidden from Llyr after Claire's death.

The scene switches again, this time to the front of the Llyr's castle and the night I ate dinner with Murphy's family. It was the first time I'd ever felt the love of a family and the first night we kissed. I watch from afar as Murphy walks around afterward, trying to settle the tension between us. I smile at the memory. The scenes playing before me are the moments of discovery. The moment I discovered my true identity. The moment I realized Llyr wasn't responsible for my childhood, and the moment I realized I loved Murphy. Why am I being shown this?

I watch as Murphy and Adria walk into the castle, arm in arm. "Dreamworld Murphy and Adria are kind of cute, aren't they?" Vita says, coming to my side. "Although, he's a little out of your league. Of course, I've always been partial to redheads. He and I had coffee once." She sighs at a memory.

"Where is he?" She's trying to upset me, and I refuse to take the bait.

She smirks. "I don't know. Like you, like everyone here, he's controlling his own world. He could be anywhere." She motions to the space around her. "You chose to come to Daddy's castle. He may be hiding out somewhere similar, who knows?"

"What are you saying?"

"Oh, come on, Adria. You're smarter than this. Figure it out." She disappears, leaving me alone in the courtyard, staring at Llyr's empty castle. The beach and ocean are gone.

She's right. I am smarter than this. Think like a goddess, Adria. I chose to come home. Maybe Murphy's stuck in a memory somewhere? I think back to the few times I talked to him. He was cold and surrounded by stone walls. Since elementals seem to hang out in ancient castles, that could be any of the places we've been. I close my eyes and visualize the last stone walls where I saw the real Murphy, the catacombs.

I'm instantly transported there, back to the image of him tied up and Lucian entering his body. I watch from a distance as the entire scene repeats. "Murphy?" I ask the memory. He doesn't respond, and Lucian walks past me sight unseen. Could his mind still be in the catacombs? No, that doesn't make any sense.

Shu would know what to do. Dammit, where is he? I focus my energy on visualizing Shu in his all white jeans and too tight sweater. "Where are you when I need you?" I call into the setting sun. I visualize the black sand beach where Llyr left this world and open my eyes to the familiar landscape. "I don't know what to do," I whisper to the sea in front of me.

"Yes, you do," it whispers back, startling me. This is another one of Vita's games. Is this real or another memory? A deep laugh echoes off the basin. "Yes, you do, my dear."

I instantly recognize the voice. "Daddy?" I ask, my voice is shaky.

"It's me. I'm sorry I can't be there in person, but my strength is limited. It's taking every bit I have to cross dimensions." Tears stream down my cheeks.

"I don't know how to get to Murphy."

"The power is inside you. You're stronger than her. That's why she's playing games with you." The sea begins to swirl in small circles not far off the beach.

"Tell me what to do."

Llyr chuckles. "I can't do that, because I don't know."

"Then what makes you think *I* do?"

"Vita has coveted our powers since the beginning of time. Everything that's happened in your life has led you here, to this moment, and nothing you could've done would change the outcome." Llyr's voice is beginning to weaken. "Find Shu. He's here, in this realm. Together, you can defeat Vita and save Murphy."

"Shu's here?"

Llyr's voice turns into nothing more than a whisper. "It's time for me to go. I love you, Adria. Find Shu."

"I love you, too," I echo toward the sea.

What the hell is Shu doing here, and how the hell am I supposed to find him? I visualize the last place I saw Shu, and immediately I'm transported back to the library of the fire castle and sitting on the sofa with my grandfather. His legs are crossed, and he's staring into the dancing flames of the fireplace. "Where are you?" I ask the image next to me. Shu slowly turns his head toward me.

"I'm doing what I have to do." He lays his hand on top of mine, and I'm transported to an ancient castle, high on top of a rocky mountain overlooking the sea. Ancient gargoyles line the roof, overlooking what lies beneath. The sea below looks similar to where I first entered the realm. Standing in front of a large door, the haze of the realm is lifted, and for the first time since arriving, I know this is real, not imaginary.

I don't bother knocking. "Honey, I'm home!" I yell, walking into the large foyer.

"Is that any way to greet an old friend?" Vita answers, stepping in front of me. She's wearing her Hannah outfit and dressed in Phoenix training gear. I laugh at the irony.

"You were never my friend."

"Poor little Adria. Orphaned and left in foster homes...blah, blah, blah. Are we going to hear this sob story again? I must tell you, it's quite boring." Her voice has a singsong tone as she mocks my childhood.

"I'm not here for you. Where's Murphy?"

Vita sighs. "Goodness. I believe you *are* having a few issues. We just had this conversation, remember? He's wherever he wants to be, and I don't know where that is."

"Maybe I can be of service." Shu walks down a grand staircase, wearing the exact outfit I imagined him in earlier. My heart sinks into my stomach. Llyr said he was here, but this is not where I expected to find him. Has he been playing me for a fool this entire time? "Hello, my dear."

"Look, she's speechless," Vita says with a laugh. "That's a rare thing these days. She never shuts up."

"Speechless isn't the word. I think murderous is closer to the correct terminology." Shu steps in front of me. I fight the tears threatening to fall. "To what do we owe the pleasure of this visit?" He smiles with his words.

"Why are you here?" My voice is no louder than a whisper.

Shu turns toward Vita. "Sowing some old oats, I guess." Vita smiles a sickening smile. She's transformed from Hannah back to the woman who made me watch my mother drown.

"Do you know where Murphy is?"

He sighs, moving to Vita's side. "No, and to be honest, I don't care." His words sting almost as much as the fact that I trusted him.

"You've been working with her this entire time, haven't you?" Anger spews from my core. "You made sure Llyr would die. You brought Murphy here—for her." I glare at the spot where Vita's taken up residence. "Hell, you even created some demonic child with her. Did you help her kill Claire?" Shu physically flinches at my last question.

His energy changes. "I would *never* hurt my child."

"She did!" I spew venom in his direction, pointing at Vita. "*She* killed your child, and you're with her, hanging out and 'sowing' your fucking oats?"

"Maybe Murphy wouldn't have left if you'd been

better at sowing yours," Vita taunts. Shu glances in her direction.

"We're finished here. I'll find him without you." I turn toward the door. "I want nothing more to do with you." I slam the heavy wooden door behind me. Vita's laughter follows me outside.

There has to be a way to find Murphy. I close my eyes, imagining the scene when I first arrived in the realm and ran into Mira. She seemed to know her way around this madness. Opening my eyes, I'm in front of a familiar home in L.A., and Mira stands in front of me.

"Hi!" she waves. I look behind her, at my last foster home before becoming a Phoenix. "You figured out how to move around," she says excitedly.

"Not really, but I'm trying." I pause. "I need some pointers."

"To find your friend?" I nod. "Okay, what do you want to know?"

"That's the problem. I don't know enough to know what I need to know." I follow her to the side of the house. She stops in front of a window, the bedroom we shared the night before I left. "Do you remember this room?"

I wipe dirt from the filthy glass. "I do."

"This isn't real. You brought us here." I nod, hoping to encourage her to continue.

"I don't remember it looking like this. I mean, it was a dump, but not this bad." Most of the windows are boarded up, and the manicured lawn has grown almost past the windows.

"It looks like this because this is what it felt like to you.

It felt dirty and destroyed, so that's how it appears in this realm."

I wrinkle my forehead. "I made it look like this?"

"Yep." She motions her hand in front of her body. "You did the same thing to me." She smiles. "We knew each other years ago. I'm much older than this now." She shudders, transforming into a teenager. "This is what I look like in my world."

"I'm sorry, I'm not following you," I admit.

Mira laughs. "It's okay, not many do, Goddess." What the what?

"Mira? Do I need to be concerned that you know what I am?"

Her smile is warm. "Not at all." She takes my hand into hers. "In this realm, there are more than five elements." She transforms again, this time into a glowing ball of light. *"I'm Mira, the Goddess of Time."* Her words echo through my mind.

CHAPTER 13

*H*oly shit. I stare blindly at the goddess in front of me. Nothing more than a ball of energy and hope. "Are you the same Mira that lived in this house?"

"Yes and no." She transforms back into the familiar face of the young girl I remember. "She was a part of me, yes, but was she completely me? No."

"I'm sorry, I don't understand."

The scenery changes to downtown L.A. and the streets I used to run as a kid. "Did you bring us here, or did I?"

"You, but I helped a little." I recognize the spot where we're standing in an instant. I used to hang out in the park across the street. Homeless people line empty doorways, reminding me of a time in my life I'd rather forget.

"Why are we here?"

"This is where you wanted to go." Mira moves in

front of a homeless man. I watch as she leans down, touching his wrists and he disappears from the scene. She does the same move for a few others nearby.

"What are you doing?"

"Giving them more time," she answers.

She continues walking through the crowd, touching people along the way, and making them disappear from this world. A familiar face is moving toward us. "Is that me?"

Mira looks up with a smile. "I think so." The Adria walking toward us is younger. Her hair is dirty and matted to her head. She's wearing clothes that are almost as dirty as her face and hair. I recognize this version immediately. This is what I looked like after being kicked out of the foster home we shared and living on the streets. "Want me to change her life?" Mira asks as she moves closer. "I can give her more time."

The light is drained from her eyes. She's tired and no doubt hungry. This is the day my life changed forever. The day that set me on the path of discovering who and what I really am. "No. The past is what makes us who we are. If I hadn't lived this moment, I wouldn't be who I am today."

"Good choice," Mira answers with a smile. "I'm a fan of learning through our experiences."

"Is that what you were doing when you were in the foster home with me?"

"In a way, yes. Sometimes an earthly experience helps ground me." Sad Adria continues moving toward us, not noticing anyone except herself. I long to reach out, touch her shoulder, and offer strength. Instead, I watch her walk past. Young, scared, and confused.

"Where would you like to go now?"

"Can you take me to Murphy? He's in this realm, trapped by Vita."

"I'm sorry, I don't know where he is. This realm is vast, and it isn't easy to find someone who doesn't want to be found."

I wipe a stray tear. "Vita's trapped him here."

We walk across the street and into the park, sitting side by side on a park bench, overlooking a very familiar lake. "I'm afraid if that's the case, I can't get to him. Each person creates their own reality in the ethereal."

"You were able to find me here."

"Yes, because a part of me shared this memory with you."

"Dammit!" I stand. "There has to be a way."

"I can't get to him, but you can." Mira stands beside me. "Not only can you manipulate your memories and jump into them, but you can manipulate time." She walks toward the lake. "I'm not sure I know how to explain this."

"Pretend you're explaining nuclear physics to a kindergarten student." Mira laughs at my words.

"I can send you in a time warp to a memory where you and Murphy are together. The memories you've experienced in this realm until now, are just that, memories. To free him from wherever he is, you'll have to break the loop of whatever memory he's trapped inside of and take him back to your realm."

"How do I get him back to our realm?" I mask the confusion from my face.

She turns, facing me. "To free him from this realm, you have to free him from Vita."

"She claims she doesn't know where he is."

"Well, she's right about not knowing, but ultimately, she's the reason he's here. Which means, she's in control of him staying and leaving."

"I'm confused," I admit.

Mira wrings her hands together. "You'll have to use your powers to get him out."

"My powers are of no use here."

"You just don't know how to connect to them."

Why does this conversation feel like it's going nowhere? "Tell me about the phoenix."

"Where did you hear that term?"

"We found mention of the phoenix of all in an ancient scroll."

She pauses in thought. "Vita is the phoenix. Figuratively, of course. She's always appeared larger than life itself, and the ethereal realm isn't immune to her ways. From a time before time, she would often appear to the other elements as a phoenix, complete with the fire. It was her way of trying to control us."

"Earlier, you said there were more than five elements in this realm. Other than earth, air, water, and fire, what is there?"

"Well, there's the big four you're familiar with, along with thunder, force, time, flower, shadow, light, and moon." I stare at her, dumbfounded. "We can't forget about aether."

"No, heaven forbid we forget about aether." I sit back on the bench.

"Earth, air, water, and fire are the primary elements, while the rest of us are considered secondary." She sits next to me. "In this realm, you are the Goddess of Earth, Fire, Water, and Air. Just like in your realm. As above, so below."

"What does that mean?"

"It means, what happens in one realm, happens in all of them."

I run my fingers through my messy hair. "So, there's a version of me here?"

"Yes." Mira stares at me as if the information she's sharing is common knowledge I should already have.

"That's the answer. Can you take me to the Adria from this realm?"

"It's not that easy." She sighs. "There can't be two versions of you in this realm."

"I'm here now."

"You two can exist in the same realm for a while, however, the longer you stay, the weaker you will become."

I stand from her side. "Then why are we wasting time talking? Take me to the me from this realm. If she's anything like me, she'll help."

"Addy isn't like you." She stands, moving to my side. "And, even if she agrees to help, you're forgetting the most important part. Getting Murphy away from Vita. Even though she doesn't have him physically, she has his soul." She turns away from the lake. "I'm sorry, I need to go. When you figure out how to retrieve your lover from Vita, call me. I'll jump you to a memory where you can grab him."

"Wait. He's running out of time..." Mira disappears in front of my eyes. Oh, my gods. This is getting more frustrating by the minute. I glance around, seeing nothing out of the ordinary. Honestly, everything's out of the ordinary, but nothing stands out. I sit on the bench, putting my head in my hands. How can I get Murphy away from Vita when I don't understand how she can keep him here and not know where he is? Every question I ask makes this more confusing than before.

Ethan is the smartest person I know, human or elemental. If anyone has answers, he will. I picture him reading the ancient scrolls in the library at Grimsgil. In an instant, I'm transported to the bowels of the castle and the now highly warded library.

Ethan's pouring through mounds of information, looking for ways to help his son. Keegan, Tempest, and Sophie are asleep, stretched out on the floor and antique chairs. I move toward Murphy's father. "Ethan." He doesn't look up. He can't hear me. "Ethan," I try again. This time he stops, looking through me into the distance. I close my eyes and focus every morsel of my energy on the human standing in front of me. "Ethan," I whisper.

"Adria?" he whispers back, looking around the small room. "Where are you?"

I focus again. "I need your help."

"That's what I'm doing," he answers. "I'm working as hard as I can."

I don't waste time with an explanation. "How can I free Murphy from Vita's hold?"

Ethan stops, looking right at me as if he can see me. "I

need more time." He continues to search through the scroll.

"Ethan?" He stops, turning toward me again. "Once I find him, how can I free him from her hold?"

"I don't need to find that information in a book. That's easy. Fight like your life and his depends on it." His answer is simple. The memory of Ethan, the library, and the park bench begins to fade into nothing, turning back into the rocky cliffs where I arrived.

"Fight." Ethan's words echo through my mind. How can I fight without the use of my powers? I close my eyes, pulling myself back to the house Mira and I shared for a week as kids. She's no older than five or six and is asleep in the room we shared. "Mira." I tap on the glass. "I need you." She appears in front of me.

"You didn't waste any time." She laughs hysterically at her comment. "Sometimes, I make myself laugh." She looks at me. "I'm the Goddess of Time, get it? It was a play on the concept of time." She clears her throat. "Never mind. Are you ready for me to jump you to your memory?"

"I know how to free him."

"Then you're ready," she answers with a smile.

"Not until you take me to Adria. The one from this realm." She frowns slightly, putting her hand on top of mine. In an instant, we're transported to a cul-de-sac that could be anywhere in America. Beautiful two-story homes surround the street, each one looking like the cover of a magazine. "Where are we?"

"The outer realm. This is where we live."

"The Gods and Goddesses of Elements live on a cul-de-sac? Do you have neighborhood cookouts and game nights, too?"

"No, but that's a great idea." I follow her to the largest house in the circle. She rings the doorbell and stands back. "I'm warning you. She's a little grumpy."

"Who?"

The door opens and an exact replica of me stands in the doorframe. "Look who the cat dragged in. What the hell do you want?"

"Hi. I'm you from…

"I know who you are," she interrupts. "What do you want?"

"I need your help."

"Why does that not surprise me?" She rolls her eyes, pissing me off.

"What can I call you?"

"That's a dumb question. My name is Adria. I am you. You are me. Call me Addy, though. Adria sounds like a shriveled-up eighty-year-old water elemental."

"You're a little prickly," I answer.

"Prickly? Is that slang for something else?"

"No. Forget I said anything." I laugh awkwardly. "I need to get to Murphy. He's running out of time." Addy shifts her hips.

"I know," she answers.

"Can you help me access my powers and get him away from Vita?"

"Vita?" I nod. "I don't know how I can help you. You should be able to access them the same way you do in your realm." Damn, the seventh-realm version of me is a bitch.

I stare at my doppelganger. "If I had access to my

powers, do you think I would have asked you for help? I can't control them in this realm, and I don't know why."

"Okay, fine." She steps toward me, touching my shoulder, and a shudder moves through my entire body. "There. See if that helps."

I turn toward a large rock on the edge of her driveway. Sending my energy to the rock, I lift it in the air without any effort.

"What did you do?"

"I fixed you." She looks bored. "What's the plan to get Murphy?"

Mira smiles. "I'm going to move her through a time warp, and you're going to help her get him away from Vita."

Addy wrinkles her forehead. "Me? I'm going to help you. I don't remember agreeing to this."

"You didn't, but I can't do it without you." She turns, walking inside the home. I look at Mira, confused at what's going on. We follow her inside the beautifully decorated home. Pale gray walls with pure white crown molding surrounds the foyer leading into the open-concept living room and dining room combination. Why does her home look like it belongs in suburban America? I stare at my twin in front of me. "I can't do this alone."

Addy is standing in the middle of the living room. She crosses her arms in front of her chest and stares at me defiantly. Her movements feel familiar. "What's in this for me?"

"A chance to save Murphy. I don't know what you've been through in this realm, and I wouldn't belittle you by trying to guess. But my life wasn't the greatest. Murphy saved me. He helped me discover who and what I am. He taught me what true love is. Now it's my turn to return the favor." My words are full of emotion.

"Okay," she whispers. "I'm tired of that bitch anyway."

CHAPTER 14

"Have a seat." She motions to a round table in the kitchen of her home. "We need a plan."

"Do you live here alone?"

"No." She doesn't elaborate.

"Did you forget about me again?" a familiar voice calls from the other side of the house.

"Tempest?"

The image of my elemental friend walks into the kitchen. He's wearing a pair of cutoff jean shorts and a white tank top. He smiles a broad, familiar smile, warming me from the inside out. He stops and stares. "You look just like Addy."

"That's because she is me," Addy answers.

He looks between the two of us. "Why am I confused?"

"You might want to sit down for this one," Addy warns. Tempest and Mira slide into the empty seats at the table. Addy sighs before explaining. "She's me from a different realm."

"A what now?" Tempest looks between the two of us.

"A different realm," I repeat Addy's words. "I'm Adria Kane, Goddess of Water, Fire, and Earth and the granddaughter of air."

Tempest thoroughly looks confused. "And, I am Addy Kane, Goddess of Water, Fire, and Earth and the granddaughter of air." She smiles from the other side of the table.

Tempest stands from his seat and bows to one knee. "My Queens. How may I be of service to you?"

"You were of service to me last night," Addy says, motioning toward Tempest. Oh, my gods. Are they a couple? Are she and Murphy not together?

"Well, this just got weird," Mira says, clapping her hands loudly. Tempest stands, clearing his throat.

The front door opens and a face I haven't seen since the battle with Astrid enters. "Peter?" I step in front of the earth elemental.

He looks between me and Addy. "What...why am I confused?"

"You just missed the introductions, Peter. You should have been here a few minutes earlier." Addy smirks as she speaks.

"Hi. I'm Adria Kane." I hold my hand toward him. He holds my hand in his as he lowers to one knee.

"My Queen," he whispers.

"You don't do that for me," Addy scoffs.

He stands, keeping his head bowed. "How may I be of service?" He turns back toward Addy. "To both of you."

"I need your help to get Murphy back to our realm. Vita has him."

Tempest looks at me like I've lost my mind. "I don't know how it is where you came from, but Vita is in charge here. We can't just walk in there and demand him back."

"No, but we can fight."

Tempest walks toward a bay window overlooking a perfectly manicured backyard. "We can, but do you know what you're asking, Goddess?"

"To be honest, no," I answer truthfully. "I have no idea what that bitch has up her sleeve, but I know I can't do it without your help. What about Keegan and Brenna? Are they nearby?"

"Keegan Jacobson?" He and Addy share a look.

"What is Keegan in your realm?" Addy asks.

I shrug. "He's an overly awkward fire hybrid genius." I look around the table, making eye contact with each. "Why is everyone acting strange?"

"Keegan was with us," Peter says, turning his eyes down with his words.

"Was? Is he dead?"

"We don't know," Addy answers. "He disappeared a while back."

"Disappeared? What does that mean?"

Tempest stands, moving toward the window. "It means he's most likely no longer alive." He doesn't elaborate, and I don't push the issue. "If he were here, he'd be first in line to help, but he's not. Jumping to the head of the line to help rescue someone was right up his alley. He loved being the hero."

"I thought what happens in one realm happens in

another. Keegan is alive and healthy in my realm. Wouldn't that mean he's alive and well here?" I turn toward Mira. "As above, so below? That's what you said."

"I did," Mira agrees.

"That's not always the case," Addy adds. "Sometimes people are gone from one realm and not the others."

I stand, walking away from the table before asking the next question. "What about Murphy?"

Addy's body language changes in an instant. "He's gone."

"You mean he's missing?"

"She means he's no longer alive," Peter answers. "He died in the battle with Astrid along with my brother." My knees weaken with his words.

"Why didn't you tell me?" I ask Addy.

"Because in your realm, he survived. You still have a chance to save your Murphy."

Tempest moves behind me, helping me find a chair without falling. "Were you two..."

"A couple?" Addy completes. "We were." She pauses. "He died trying to save Llyr." She pauses. "It's why I agreed to help you save your Murphy, and it's why Vita's been able to hold him here in this realm. There can be only one."

"Are you two together?" I ask, looking between Addy and Tempest.

Addy sighs. "After Murphy...after he died, Tempest was here for me. Things just kind of escalated. I guess you could say we're a couple."

"Murphy was my best friend," Tempest adds.

"I'm so sorry. You lost Llyr and Murphy the same

day?" She nods. No wonder she's a little bitchy. She earned it.

"How many realms are there?" I ask the group sitting around me.

"Seven," Mira answers.

"If there is a version of Adria in each realm, why is Vita determined to come after me? What about the other realms?"

"We're all that's left," Addy answers.

I stare wide-eyed. "Only two Adria's remain?"

"Yes," she answers.

"Then we have to fight."

"Yes, we do," she agrees.

Mira claps her hands again, making me jump. "Okay, team. How are we going to get Murphy back to Adria's realm? I can handle getting her to him in time, but we need a plan to get them home."

"There's only one way to do this. We're going to kick some ass." Addy stands, moving away from the table.

"What about Lucian?" I ask.

"What about that piece of shit. He's nothing but a good-for-nothing wannabe mama's boy."

"You know who his mother is?" I ask.

"Of course. He wears it on his sleeve like a badge of honor." She stands very straight, making a strange face. "My mother is the Goddess of Aether," she mimics Lucian's voice, pretending to be him. "I'll invade your dreams and pretend to be a vampire."

"Sounds about right." I laugh. "But I'm afraid there's more to the story." Everyone's eyes turn to me. I sigh before continuing. "There's a strong possibility that Shu is his father."

The group stares at me dumbfoundedly. "Are you fucking serious?" Addy asks. I raise my eyebrows and nod. "He's the son of the Goddess of Aether and the God of Air?"

"What does that mean?" Peter asks.

"It means he's more powerful than anyone knows," Tempest answers.

Addy moves to the couch and sits heavily. "There are different versions of each of us in every realm. Which means, originally, there were seven versions of Adria. However, Vita and Lucian only exist on this realm. There are no others. They move freely throughout the realms, going wherever they choose." She curses under her breath. "The whole reason she brought Murphy here was to get you to this realm. It's the reason why my Murphy died. This has been her plan the entire time."

"I'm here, and I'm not leaving without him," I answer.

"That's what she's hoping for." Tempest moves to an antique desk, pulling something from one of the drawers. "These are the blueprints of her castle. Don't ask me how I have them, and to be honest, they may not be accurate." He opens the plans on top of the kitchen table we surrounded moments earlier. "Murphy's soul will have to be freed before he can truly escape. He's most likely being held here." I move to his side to see he's pointing at a blank spot on the blueprint.

"What is that?"

"The void."

I shake my head. "No. I've been in the void thousands of times looking for him. He's not there. If he were, I would've found him already."

"Your realm's version of the void is a shadow of the void on this realm." Addy moves to my side. "In this realm, the void is whatever Vita wants it to be. It's what gives Lucian his power to invade dreams and Vita the power to change each realm." She points to the same spot. "This is how Vita moves from realm to realm, freely. This is where his soul will be, and this is where we'll have to fight."

"What about the other gods and goddesses in this realm? Mira said there are more. Maybe they would help us?"

Addy laughs. "They won't be any help. Most of them are in hiding and scared of her. We're all that we've got."

I nod. "Mira, tell me what to do."

"Think of a memory where I can transport you physically back in time. You have the power to move freely through those memories as an observer, which is what you've been doing since you arrived here. While you're there, I can alter time and allow you to be a participant in the memory for a brief moment. When that happens, you have to pull Murphy with you, and the two of you will return here."

"Like physically grab onto him? Sounds easy enough." Tempest shifts his weight.

"I need to warn you," she continues. "You are only bringing his vessel. He will have the memories, language, and knowledge of Murphy, but he won't *be* Murphy. As soon as his body leaves your memory, he'll be nothing more than an empty vessel."

"Because his soul is in Vita's void?"

"Yes."

"This is sounding better by the moment," Addy says. Her sarcasm reminds me of myself.

"Will he fight with us?" Peter asks.

"Maybe? We won't know until we get him here." Mira smiles.

"And if he won't come willingly?" I ask.

"Then we force him to regain his soul. We can't get the soul without the body. In order to leave the void, the soul must have a vessel."

"He has a vessel in my realm," I answer.

"There can only be one. Once you retrieve his soul, place it in the new vessel, and return him to your realm, the vessel in your realm will die." Everyone stares at Mira.

"How do you know all of this?" Addy asks.

Mira shrugs. "It's the magic of time. Adria, think of your memory, and we'll go."

I close my eyes, clear my mind, and think of our first kiss. After meeting his parents for the first time, we walked back to Llyr's castle and shared a kiss. It was magical and goosebumps cover my arms with the memory. I pull on the emotions flowing through my body, allowing them to surround me. "Okay," I whisper.

"I see it," Mira answers, taking my hand into hers, we're transported to the ancient bridge on the Isle of Man. Murphy's standing in front of me, wearing the tight jeans that I teased him about. He's smiling, and our emotions are running high. I merge into the Adria from my memory, and the scene continues.

I fight the overwhelming urge to cry with the emotions I'm experiencing. Seeing the fragile, empty vessel and comparing it to the strong, virile man standing in front of me is almost more than I can handle.

Murphy steps toward me, sliding one hand to my cheek and the other to my waist. Every crash of the sea, the caw of a seagull, crickets singing their song, resonates deep inside. His eyes move to my lips, and he slowly moves his head toward mine.

My eyes close with the memory. *I turn my head to the side, giving him more access. My lips part as he gently touches my tongue with his.*

Oh, gods. Murphy, I'm so sorry I let this happen to you. I should've stopped her. *The arm around my waist slides to my back and under the hem of the sweater. His skin touching mine brings even more heat. I slide my hands underneath the ridge of his jeans to touch his skin. Our kisses turn desperate.*

"Now!" Mira yells from nowhere, interrupting the scene in front of me. Every fiber of my being wants to stay here, with him, in this moment. I grab hold of his waist, pulling him tightly as Mira pulls us to the cul-de-sac, and to the seventh realm, together.

Murphy steps away from me. "What's going on?" He looks around the contemporary home, resting his eyes on Tempest, Peter, Addy, and Mira. "Who are you?" He loses his footing, falling on all fours. "Where I?" He's scared, and his fear shows across his face.

"We need your help," I say, pulling him to a standing position.

"I don't know you." His voice and actions remind me of a scared child.

"Didn't you say he'd have his memories?" Addy whispers to Mira.

"It was more of a theory, really," she answers.

"How much more of this was a theory?" Tempest asks. Mira doesn't answer, just smiles. "That's what I was afraid of."

"What do you want with me?" Murphy asks. This version of Murphy is nothing more than a healthier version of the vessel lying on a makeshift hospital bed in Iceland, only this one is conscious. "Who are you?"

"What are we going to do with him?" Addy asks.

"We have to take him with us. The soul must have a vessel," Mira reminds us.

"I'm not going anywhere with you!" Murphy becomes combative, swinging at Tempest.

"Easy there, buddy." Tempest moves away from his swing. "We're here to help you."

Addy hits Murphy in the temple hard enough to knock him out. He falls to the ground with a thud. "Was that necessary?" I ask, moving to his side.

"Very," she answers. "Let's go."

"Where?" I wipe the blood from Murphy's face.

"To Vita's, of course." Addy places her hand on my shoulder, and the five of us jump to the mountainous seaside cliffs where I first entered this realm.

CHAPTER 15

*T*empest gently places Murphy's vessel on the ground. "He's going to be heavy to carry to the castle."

"Agreed, but he won't be able to make the trip conscious. He's nothing more than a confused bag of bones. It's better for him to be knocked out." Addy's words are laced with anger. Tempest sighs, bending to pick Murphy back up.

"I can help." I send a blast of air to Murphy, lifting his body off the ground several feet. "I need something to wrap around him, and we can pull him with us. No one will have to carry him."

Mira smiles, unwrapping a sash she's had tied around her waist. "Here, you can use this." I tie the sash around Murphy's torso and use it like a lasso.

"How do you control the elements like that?" Addy asks.

I shrug. "The same way you do, I suppose."

"I don't have control over any of the elements. I'm the Goddess, just like you, and have aspects of them all, but I can't control any of them. Not in the way that you can, apparently."

I stare at the seventh-realm version of me. "You fixed my powers. How were you able to do that and not control the elements?"

She shrugs. "That's the one thing I *can* do. I can strengthen elemental gifts. Just not my own." I stare at her, not sure what to say. "Don't look at me like that. It's the way it's always been. I guess that's why Vita has left me alone. I'm no use to her. It's why I couldn't save Llyr or Murphy." She starts walking, carrying her anger and sadness with her.

I follow Addy, Mira, Peter, and Tempest, tugging Murphy along behind. No one speaks as we make our way across the rocky terrain. We don't have a plan, and I'm not sure we could come up with one, even if we tried. All I know is we're going to have to fight. "How much further to the castle?" My words sound like a child whining from the backseat of a car on a long road trip.

"A few more miles," Tempest answers.

"Before we get closer, can we discuss some sort of plan? I feel like we're heading into battle with no clue of what to expect." I stop walking, pulling Murphy to a stop with me.

"We could do that, but the truth is, none of us have any clue what's waiting for us. Vita's in charge of this realm, which means she already knows we're coming."

"Then why the hell are we taking our time? Why not just jump there and start kicking ass?" I look into the eyes of each member of our small group. "We're wasting time that Murphy doesn't have."

On cue, energy fills the air around us. I recognize the energy instantly, even before he appears. In front of me stands my grandfather, Shu.

"Because we were waiting on his slow ass," Addy says, wrinkling her upper lip. "Don't fall for his tricks. He's not like the Shu you think you know. This one's a piece of shit who traded his family for power." She turns away from her grandfather.

"I thought we were over all of that," Shu says, straightening his suit coat. Unlike Shu from my realm, this Shu is dressed in a black three-piece suit. His shirt and tie are monochrome and the same color as his hair and eyes. He looks me up and down. "Well, this is a strange conundrum."

"I'm Adria," I answer.

"You don't say?" His voice is laced with sarcasm. "I'm glad you cleared that up for me. I'm guessing you aren't from around here?" I haven't felt this judged since middle school.

"Why were we waiting on him?" I ask our small group.

Addy laughs. "She's already figured you out."

"You're waiting because I know how to get into Vita's castle," Shu answers.

"How did you contact him?" I'm so confused right now.

"Carrier pigeon," Addy answers. She's beginning to piss me off. She has every right to be angry, but when it affects my ability to save Murphy, that's where I draw the line.

"Addy, I'm sorry that your Murphy is dead and that your powers are different from mine, but you're going to have to tell me what's going on. Why and how did you contact Shu to get directions on the castle? I need to know everything."

She sighs, squinting her eyes at me. "I contacted him telepathically."

I stare at Addy confused. "That's something you can do?"

"Yes. Can't you?"

I don't answer. "Do we trust him?" I ask, turning back toward the Shu dressed in black.

"No, we don't. But we don't have any other options," Tempest answers.

Shu moves closer to Murphy. "All this is for him?" He points to Murphy, floating and tied to a sash. "What's so special about him?"

I don't answer. Addy's right, this version of Shu sucks, even more than the one currently shacked up with Vita in her castle. "How are you getting us inside?"

Shu laughs. "I'm not going with you. I'm just pointing the way." He moves next to Addy, handing her a small device.

"What's this?" she asks.

"It's a map of the castle."

"We have the blueprints. We don't need a map. We need inside," she retorts.

"The blueprints aren't correct. If you follow them, you'll walk right into her next trap."

"Why should we trust you?" Addy stares angrily at Shu.

"Because if you don't, you'll die." He walks away from our group. "The choice is yours." He straightens his tie before jumping away from our view.

Addy holds the device to the sky, looking through the clear screen that resembles something from Star Trek. "Did you bring the blueprints?" Tempest pulls them from a bag around his shoulders, opening them on the rocks. She looks between the two a few times. "Shit. They're different."

"Do we trust him or the blueprints?" Tempest asks.

"We trust him," Mira answers. "He's being truthful, and this device is correct."

"How are you so sure?" Addy asks, sliding the device into her pocket.

"I've seen Shu through time. He regrets his past and sees this as a way to make up for what's happened."

"It's going to take a lot more than this to make up for all the shit he put me through." Addy has stories that I wish I had time to hear.

"This is a good start," Mira defends Shu.

"He still didn't help us get inside," Peter reminds the group.

"I can help with that." I form a wall of protection, hiding us from the outside world. "Now we're invisible." The small group looks around the bubble.

Addy raises her eyebrows. "That comes in handy. Let's go." We make our way through the rough terrain, hidden from outside eyes. The top of the castle comes into view as we approach, and a thick fog surrounds the perimeter, making it resemble something from a horror movie. "Even though we're hidden, she knows we're here. I'm sure of it."

"Are we just going to sit out here and wait for her to invite us inside?" The last time I felt this unprepared for battle, Llyr died. I don't like this.

"She'll come to us. After the fight, we'll get inside and to the void." Addy takes charge and, surprisingly, I let her. Within minutes, a sound rushes toward us from the castle. "Here she comes. That was quicker than I thought. Whatever you do, don't release our protective disguise."

Tempest steps closer to Addy. "Can you give me a boost?" She nudges him on the shoulder, and instinctively, I know she's strengthened his elemental power. The sound of flapping wings echoes off the castle's stone facade.

"What's that sound?" I ask our small group.

"Vita," Addy answers.

"Is she an actual phoenix?" I stare toward the source of the sound.

"Probably. She's been known to do that a time or two," Tempest answers.

"I thought you said she was a figurative phoenix?" I ask Mira, who smiles and shrugs. Moments later glimpses of something large flying toward us, appears over the horizon. "That's a damn phoenix!" Brightly colored feathers glisten in the sunlight and give off a metallic green glow. She's both terrifying and beautiful at the same time.

"Are you sure your shields are working? She's heading right for us!" Addy asks. I reinforce the shields, pushing as much energy as I can spare into our protection. "Hold on!" Addy shouts over the roaring wind. The five of us are picked up and jump straight to the castle gates and small courtyard at the entrance. "Drop the shield!" Addy yells. I do, and the phoenix appears, circling overhead and heading straight toward us.

"Shit," Mira whispers.

"Stand your ground." Tempest moves to the front of our group and turns into a twenty-foot wall of water. Peter moves beside him, forming an even larger tornado.

The phoenix drops to the ground in front of us, making the ground shake with her landing. *"Hello there."* Her words project through each of our minds. *"I hoped you two would find each other. I feel like a proud mother."*

"Why don't you fight face to face?" I yell toward the giant creature.

"This is my true face," she mocks. *"Your grandfather seems to like it."*

"Eww," Addy says what I'm thinking.

Vita transforms into the familiar shape of the woman from the beach. "Let's talk then." She sits on a large boulder and smirks, seeing Murphy tied to a sash and floating behind me. "Come on girls. Let's have a chat." She pats each side of her, asking us to join her on the boulder. "Oh, relax. You two are always ready to fight everything. If all I wanted was a fight, I wouldn't have gone through all the trouble of getting you two together."

Addy and I share a look. "You didn't *get* us together," I spew.

Vita laughs loudly. "Are you kidding me? This is the crux of my masterpiece! You two are the last ones left. Do you know how long I've planned this?"

"Do we care?" Addy asks me.

"Not really." I shrug.

"I'll admit, the others weren't as talented as the two of you, but they were still fun." Vita stands from the boulder. "But it's time to finish this. I need your powers."

"Why do you need our powers? Aren't you the most powerful elemental of any realm? Why do you need ours?" Addy steps away from me, ready for whatever Vita's about to do. Tempest and Peter are still in elemental form, and Mira's standing next to them ready to fight. All three are prepared for whatever's about to happen.

"Because I can't be the strongest while the two of you are still out there, mucking things up throughout the universe, can I?" Vita turns back into the phoenix in the blink of an eye. *"However, I'm bored with this."* A blast of fire shoots from seemingly nowhere, landing feet away from where Murphy's vessel is lying. How the hell is he still unconscious? Using air, I push his body, hiding it behind a stack of smaller rocks, and cover him with a shield to keep the vessel hidden. Combining all elements, I lift off the ground, making myself even with the phoenix.

"You're not the only one bored with this!" I shout at the monster. "You've made my life a living hell from day one." I send a blast of energy straight into her core, knocking her back a few feet. I follow it up with a second shot, and again, she falls back slightly.

"There you go. Let's get this over with," Vita mocks. *"Tap into that baggage you carry on your shoulders and use it to fight me. It'll make it more fun for both of us."*

Addy moves to the other side of Vita. "Don't let her get to you. She's trying to make you mad, make you do dumb things. Ignore the bitch." Thankfully, Addy moves faster than Vita's flames, and she jumps out of the line of fire. Tempest jumps in front of the fire, extinguishing it immediately.

Peter moves in front of her, pushing her with his wind, while I move to the other side, hitting her with a blast like before. She barely moves. *"Is this all you've got?"* She flies higher in the sky. *"I had such high hopes for the two of you."*

Fire hits Peter's storm, and he instantly turns into something from nightmares, a swirling fire tornado. I pull on the energy of water, hitting him with a full blast of water. His human form collapses to the ground in a heap of charred clothes and smoke. Vita turns her attention to Mira, who's watching from below. She slaps Mira with a wing, knocking her at least a hundred yards away from our fight.

"Mira!" I shout after her. She lands, unconscious, on a pile of stones. Oh, my gods. I turn back toward the giant phoenix. "That's enough, bitch." Pulling every bit of energy inside myself, I blow it straight toward Vita. It hits her with enough force that she flies backward, hitting the side of the castle. Like an image from a cartoon, she slides to the ground, sits up, shakes her head, and lifts off the ground.

"That was better."

"I don't need your approval," I bark at her.

"We both know that's not true, don't we? Your whole life has been about seeking love and approval. That's the root of all your issues if you ask me." She stalks closer. *"It's what makes you weak. You had such potential, but you wasted it*

on such futile things." Peter and Mira are still unconscious as Addy and Tempest stalk closer to the phoenix.

"Love isn't futile. Just because you've never felt love or had someone love you unconditionally doesn't mean I'm weak for wanting it."

"I've felt love before. It was boring. I'd rather feel power, and right now, I want yours." Instead of attacking me, she moves closer to Peter, hitting him with a blast of fire. Tempest moves toward him, putting the flames out before they do more damage to his already injured body.

"You're a coward!" I shout. "You can't fight me as Vita or Hannah or whoever the hell you pretend to be for the moment. That makes you weak!"

A deep laugh rumbles through my mind. *"I don't have to pretend to be anyone because I am everyone!"* A blast of fire shoots from her body, this time hitting Mira.

"No!" I shout and jump to her side. I form a protective shield, hiding us from her blast.

The world around me slows to nothing more than a snail's pace. One glance at Mira and I understand why. She's barely standing with her arms lifted high above her head. A large ball of energy forms between her hands, circling around her body faster than my eyes can track. "They're coming," she pants, breathing harder.

"Who's coming?" Chill bumps cover my arms and legs at the rush of energy heading toward us. I don't recognize what I'm feeling. Shit! We're barely hanging on now. We can't fight anyone or anything else. Mira grunts, pulling her hands further away from one another, making the ball grow and intensify. Blood drips from the corners of her eyes and nostrils as she continues to grow the spinning ball between her hands. Time stops completely, locking Vita in its grip.

"I can't...hold it," she grunts, clearly in pain. Two shapes land between the now-frozen phoenix and us. One is the color of lightning and glows through the sky. The other is nothing more than a wisp of constantly moving shadow.

"Release her!" The shadow shouts through our minds. Mira releases Vita and collapses to the rocks below.

"This looks slightly familiar," Vita mocks through our minds. *"Although, you're missing a few friends. I thought you learned your lesson last time."*

"We're not afraid of you," a deeper voice replies.

Vita scoffs. *"Looks like most of you are."* She shoots a blast of fire into the shadow energy, throwing him a few yards backward. He's back at our side in an instant. She tries the same move with the glowing energy, pushing him back slightly.

"We're not leaving this time, Vita," the deep voice speaks again. *"We abandoned her before. We will not do it again."* He moves next to Addy.

Mira and Peter are back on their feet. Mira turns into a glowing ball, moving closer to her friends. Along with Addy, the four of them lift off the ground, side by side, facing the monster. I join them, adding my energy to theirs.

Vita's laugh echoes off the basin. *"Fools, all of you. I thought better of you two. However, you've disappointed me, just like all the others."*

A wall of water and a swirling storm form next to us as Tempest and Peter join our fight.

"We're slow learners," the deep voice of the glowing energy answers.

"They say the first step to accepting our failure is understanding what the weakness is. You've taken the first step." Vita takes a deep breath in, preparing to blast all of us with one wall of fire. I form a shield between us and the phoenix, blocking the blow she's about to send our way.

"Join your powers with me!" I shout to my new friends. They don't hesitate, and I feel the rush of power hit me instantly. Combining my elements with theirs, along with the boost from Addy, fills my body with more power than I've ever felt. Every part of my body is alive. I corral the energy threatening to erupt, focusing every bit of it on the creature in front of us.

The power explodes, hitting her in the chest and knocking her to the ground in a thunderous crash. Rocks fly high from the impact crater left in her wake. Her body transforms back to the familiar human form, and she gasps for air, trying to fill her human lungs.

The five of us land, surrounding the weakened Goddess of Aether, and form a circle around her body. The shadow energy transforms into a young man with dark black hair and olive-colored skin. He's wearing all black and breathing hard but looks uninjured. The lightening colored energy shifts into an older man who looks around the same age as Llyr and Shu. He's wearing what looks like a toga, reminding me of the textbook image of a Greek god.

"Tie her up," the older man orders. The shadow energy pulls a rope from somewhere magical, binding her hands and feet. Toga man tears a piece of fabric from his clothes, wrapping it around her eyes and mouth.

Tempest and Peter transform back to human form, moving on either side of me. "I thought both of you left," Peter questions our helpers.

"We did," the younger one answers. "But we came back."

"Why?" Addy steps in front of the dark-haired shadow. "You abandoned us at the battle for Grimsgil. Now, you return?"

The younger man shifts from foot to foot. "We were wrong."

"Murphy and Llyr died. Your being there could've prevented that from happening. Where were you?" She is full of anger.

"We were wrong for leaving," the older man answers. "We know that now."

"A lot of good that does Llyr or Murphy." Addy turns away from the newcomers.

"Addy, I'm sorry. You and I both know that we wouldn't have been any help during that battle." The older man moves in front of her. "Their fates were decided long before we fought. There was nothing any of us could have done to change that fate. That's not how this works."

Addy wipes a stray tear, looking back at the tied-up phoenix. "That's not true. Her Murphy is alive. He could still be alive," her voice fades to a whisper.

"They're right, Addy." Mira moves to her side. "I've watched the battle through many different times. It always ends the same."

"Why'd yours get to live," Addy spews toward me.

I stare at the broken woman in front of me. "You may not have been able to save him in this realm, but you can save him in another."

"Why do you get to ride off in the sunset with the love of your life and...and I don't?"

I move toward my twin, wrapping my arms around her and pulling her close. "I don't have an answer." Addy buries her head in my shoulder for a brief moment, before pulling back.

The older man extends his hand toward me. "I'm Mellan, God of Lightning." I shake his hand, feeling incredibly awkward.

"Adria Kane, Goddess of Earth, Fire, and Water and granddaughter of air."

Mellan turns to Addy, "Looks like we have some catching up to do."

She scoffs. "That's an understatement."

The younger man steps forward. "I'm Kage, God of Shadow. It's a pleasure to meet you, Adria Kane."

In a moment, ripped from the pages of my father's death on the beach, Vita sits up, ripping the bindings from her body. She remains in human form, rising high into the sky. Her skin glows, sending waves of light through her eyes, mouth, and nose. "I have spent count-less millennia preparing for this moment. You will not take it away from me." An ear-piercing roar leaves her throat, reminding me of an old Godzilla movie. She moves straight toward me and Addy as we stand side by side in disbelief. "Do you know how hard it was to plan both of your parents' deaths simultaneously and then pretend to be your friends?" She moves higher in the sky. "You have no respect for my power and that offends me." She begins spinning in circles, slow at first then speeding up until she's moving so fast, she's nothing more than a blur of light.

Addy and I instinctively join hands. Guided by something more powerful than us, we speak in unison.

"We are the Goddesses of Four Elements and blood of two. Together, we send you back to the hell from which you came." Pure white light energy flows from our connection and into the demon floating above us. The moment our light hits her, any source of life fades from her eyes, and her body collapses with a thud on the rocks below.

The group of gods and goddesses stare blankly at what remains of Vita's vessel. Addy turns to me. "Was that you, or did I help somehow?"

"It was definitely both of us."

"My powers aren't like yours. How could I have combined power with you?" She holds her hands in front of her face.

"Your power is to boost elemental powers," Mellan says, moving closer to Vita's body. "Your boost gave Adria the strength she needed to kill Vita, for good." I stare at the remains of the woman that's terrorized me from childhood. What remains looks nothing like her. The body is shriveled, small, and on the verge of disintegrating.

"We can't leave her here, can we?" Mira asks, moving to her side.

"She would leave us." Addy turns toward the castle. "This is far from over." She points at the silhouette of a man, running in the direction of the looming building.

His hands are tied behind his back, and he's stumbling, but he's on the move.

"Shit," I whisper. Murphy's vessel is awake and heading straight for the castle. "I'll get him," I lift off the ground, flying above his head and landing in front of him.

He stops with a startle. "Leave me alone!"

"I can't do that." He backs away, stumbling over his own feet.

"You killed her!" he nods to where Vita's body lays on the rock.

"We did, but we're not done. We need you." I reach toward him, and he recoils. I sigh before continuing. "There is a very important part of you inside the castle. Without it, you're going to die."

"What the hell are you talking about?"

"Your soul is not inside your body." I don't waste time.

"What?" he asks. "That's impossible."

"You're nothing more than a walking, talking shell of a person. Your soul, Murphy's soul is trapped inside of that castle." I point behind me for dramatic effect.

"Plenty of soulless people live long fruitful lives," he retorts. He frees his hands from the meager ties and pulls a knife from his boot.

"That's not how this is going to go, Murphy. No one is going to hurt you. You're the reason we're here." I hold my hands in front of me, hoping to settle his movements.

"No! Leave me alone. I don't believe you," he yells.

"Shut the hell up," Addy says from behind, knocking Murphy unconscious again.

"He's going to have brain damage if you keep doing that!"

"You were never going to talk him into any kind of plan, and his soul is running out of time. Arguing with a blank canvas isn't getting you anywhere." The rest of the gods move behind her.

"What's our plan?" Kage asks.

"We find his soul and send them back to where they belong." Addy sheaths a knife in a thigh holster and turns to the small group. "This isn't your fight. None of you have to do this."

"We know," Mellan answers. "We're here because we want to be. We won't desert you again." I tie Mira's sash around Murphy's vessel, and the seven of us work our way toward the castle.

CHAPTER 16

The castle is only a few hundred yards ahead. The closer we get, the larger it looks. "Are we just going to walk in?" Kage asks.

"No, we'll knock first," Mira answers with a smirk.

"Goddess, we have no idea what's waiting on the other side," Tempest speaks for the first time in a while. "There could be thousands of lessers waiting behind those doors."

"Except there won't be," Mellan answers. "Vita's too arrogant to have anyone help her." He nods to the castle. "My guess is that it's nothing more than an empty shell."

"Shu was here earlier," I add and stop walking. "He was in the castle with her."

"Of course, he was." Addy's voice reeks of sarcasm. "He's going to be wherever is most convenient and advantageous for him at the time. Shu's main point of concern is Shu."

"Not your version of Shu. The one from my realm." The rest of the group turns to face me.

"That's a different story. How was he here?" Mira asks.

"I don't know, but it was my Shu. I'm sure of it."

We continue to the front door of the castle. Kage's loud knocks echo through the room on the other side. Not sure what might be waiting, I cover our group with a shield, protecting us from any traps that might be waiting. Peter steps in front and kicks the door open.

"Hello!" Addy yells into the emptiness. Her voice ricochets through the castle with no response. "Come out, come out, wherever you are!" she continues. There are no sounds, no anything.

The moment I step through the threshold, my stomach twists as if I've been punched in the gut. "Adria?" Addy's voice rings through my ears. "What's going on?"

I collapse on the floor, watching, as the room spins, unable to respond. Above me, flashing lights form, resembling stars on a clear night. The stars fade, and I'm pulled into inky darkness.

"Adria!" Mira's voice is the last thing I hear before my world goes dark.

My eyes open to the makeshift hospital room at the fire castle. What the hell? I sit up as the spinning slows. "Adria?" Bonnie's voice calls from behind. "Are you back?"

"I'm not sure." I slide out of the bed my body was sharing with Murphy's vessel. "Is this real?"

Bonnie rushes to my side. "Oh, dear. Ethan!" she shouts. "Come quickly." Bonnie wraps her short arm around my waist, helping me move to a chair not far from the bed. Ethan and Sophie rush into the room, flanking either side of me.

"What's happened?" Sophie asks.

"I don't know. Give me a minute." On the other side of the room, Murphy's vessel is breathing in short, ragged spurts. "What's wrong with him?"

"His body is failing," Bonnie answers. "It's only a matter of time now." Her words are barely more than a whisper.

"Have you found his soul?" Sophie doesn't waste time.

"Not yet, but Vita is dead."

Ethan moves from my side. "Vita is dead?"

"I'll explain later. Right now, I need to get back. We were heading into Vita's castle to find Murphy's soul when I somehow returned here." I stand, feeling more like myself. "Ethan, I have to get back, now. You have to help me."

"Murphy's body is weakening. The connection to his soul is weakening," Brenna announces, walking into the room. "I don't think his vessel is strong enough to use as a portal."

"Tell me how to get back!" I shout. "We were almost there!" Panic fills my voice.

"Maybe we can help." Keegan runs in from another room with Tempest right on his heels. "I've been researching since you left. From what I've gathered, you can borrow our power long enough to jump back to the ethereal realm."

"Tell me how." I don't question Keegan's knowledge.

"How do you know this will work?" Ethan asks. "I've

poured over countless hours of scrolls and books and barely found any information."

"It took some digging, but I found some information on realms buried deep in the dark web," Keegan answers.

"Whatever you do, do it quickly." I nod at the empty vessel behind me. "He's out of time."

Keegan takes control. "Everyone, form a circle around Adria." He turns to Sophie. "Can you please get Rhys? We'll need his power, too." Sophie runs from the room without question. "Ethan, Bonnie, could you both lay your hands on Murphy's shoulders? He's not conscious, but maybe the support of his family will give him a little boost that will help." They do as directed as Sophie runs back into the room, dragging Rhys behind her.

"Your Highness?" he questions.

"I need all the elementals to form a circle around Adria and hold hands. Tempest, you and I will hold onto Murphy." Everyone moves quickly, not questioning his orders. They form a small circle, encasing me inside.

"Now, tap into your elemental power, and instead of using it, send it through our joined connection and toward Adria."

"Are you sure this is going to work?" Brenna asks, wrapping a hand around Rhys's.

"No," Keegan admits. "But it's our only choice. Adria?" He turns toward me. "Whatever you did to get there last time, do the same thing. With the combination of our shared power and yours, this theoretically should work."

I look around the room at my family. "I love you all." I close my eyes as the rush of their power enters my body. "I feel it." Flashes of the people I love fill my mind as images of Murphy, Llyr, Brenna, Keegan, Tempest, Bonnie, Ethan, Sophie, and even Shu appear.

"Save him," Bonnie's words are the last thing I hear as I picture Vita's castle and my new friends, risking their lives to save Murphy's soul. My world goes black, and my eyes open to the front of Vita's castle just as Peter kicks the door in.

"Hello!" Addy yells into the emptiness. Her voice ricochets through the castle with no response. "Come out, come out, wherever you are!" she continues. Oh, my gods. It worked! I'm back at the exact moment I left.

I move into the castle, looking around the vast expanse and making sure I'm not hallucinating. "This *is* Vita's castle, right?" I ask my doppelganger.

"What the hell are you talking about?" Addy answers.

"Never mind." I smile and join back in the search. I owe Keegan a huge raise and a hug.

Mellan climbs the bottom few steps of the grand staircase. "We need to stay together. There's strength in numbers."

"Where's that tablet?" Tempest asks. Addy pulls it from a pocket, holding it up to a dimly lit torch.

"What's this?" Kage takes it from her.

"It's a map of the castle." I point to a blank area on the screen. "This is where Murphy's soul is." Kage wrinkles his forehead and shrugs.

"Why do we care?" he asks. I stare at the young man dressed in black, not sure how to answer.

"Don't be a dick, Kage," Addy says, moving up the

stairs. "Just because you didn't get along with Murphy doesn't mean we shouldn't help her."

"I'm fine with helping her. It's *him* I'm not a fan of helping." I don't ask for an explanation, as I follow Addy to the landing. She holds the tablet in front of her, catching the light from another flame. Studying the picture, she turns down a long hallway.

I send my energy throughout the castle, searching for anything familiar, finding nothing. Murphy's vessel is still unconscious and floating behind me. Our group makes its way through the narrow halls, past priceless antiques, and ancient tapestries. Murphy's foot bumps off the edge of a small table, knocking a small box to the floor. Everyone stops moving and faces me.

"Sorry," I whisper. The further we walk, the darker the hall becomes.

"Where's a fire elemental when you need one?" Kage asks, trying to light an old cigarette lighter. I create flames on my hands, sending light down the hallway and lighting every torch along the way.

"That's useful," Mellan says, moving to the front of our line.

"According to this," Addy points at the tablet. "The void is through that door." We surround the door, not sure if this is another one of her traps.

"I'll go," I look around our group. "I've been to the void thousands of times."

"What does that have to do with anything?" Addy asks. "Mel's right. We need to stick together."

"We'll be ripped away from each other as soon as we enter. That's exactly what the void is. It's a place where everything and nothing exists simultaneously. It's the place where nightmares live." I step toward the door. "I'm doing this alone. I won't let you put yourselves in danger for me or for Murphy." I enter the room, pulling the vessel beside me before anyone has a chance to protest.

The complete lack of everything instantly takes my breath away. There are no walls, floors, or ceilings. I'm floating in a room of nothing with the vessel tethered to my waist. This is one gigantic sensory deprivation tank. "Murphy!" I scream into the nothingness. My voice doesn't echo, it simply leaves my lips.

I pull on the sash, moving the vessel closer. "Come on, bud. We need to find your soul." I move through the void, or at least I feel like I'm moving. With the way this place works, I'm probably walking in place. "Do you feel anything?" I ask the unconscious vessel of my boyfriend. A flicker of light catches my attention ahead. Great, now I'm delusional.

"Murphy!" I call into the void. The flicker of light grows as I continue moving. "We're getting closer to whatever that is." I lower my voice, not sure what if anything is ahead. It's not until I'm in front of the candle that I realize it's nothing more than a single candle, sitting inside of an old-fashioned candelabra that appears to be floating in the air.

"Hello?" There's a note tied to the base of the candle. *Thought you might be able to use this,* the note reads. I look for the author, finding no one. "Dammit, this is pointless." I can't find him without some sort of energy to latch on to.

"Did you like my gift?" a deep voice calls through the

nothing. I startle at the sound. "I picked it out with you in mind." The voice feels familiar. Pulling Murphy's vessel closer, I turn in circles, searching for the source. "I see you still scare easily." He laughs, and I recognize the timbre of the voice instantly.

"What do you want, Lucian?"

He moves into the shadows cast by the dim candle. He's wearing his signature top hat and long black coat and carrying a walking stick. "Hello, Adria. Long time, no see."

"I was okay with that." I try focusing a shield around Murphy and me, forgetting I have very little control over my elements in the void. Shit.

"Mother will be so pleased you stopped by." He doesn't know Vita's dead.

"I hate that I won't be seeing her anymore." I smile, knowingly.

He steps closer to Murphy. "What do we have here?" A long pointy boot nudges Murphy's side.

"What do you want, Lucy?"

He laughs. "Lucy? I haven't been called that in... centuries. Mother called me that when I was younger."

"Hard to imagine you being young."

"Oh, I was young once. We hybrid's age, just much slower than our human counterparts." He smiles, stepping further into the light. "Mother would take me everywhere with her." He sits in an imaginary chair. "Yes, in case you're wondering, that meant into each realm at will. I guess that's where my love of visiting others came from."

"Don't you mean that's where your love of stalking people in their dreams came from?"

He nods. "I guess that's one way to put it." A steaming teacup appears in his hand, and he takes a sip. "How rude of me. Would you care for a cup of tea?" A second one appears.

"How do you do that?" He looks confused at my question.

"Do what? Make tea?"

"You're sitting on an invisible chair and drinking tea that appeared from nowhere. How did you do that?"

He stands. "Oh, that. What you see as nothing, I see as everything." He sets the cup on the table from earlier. "You see, the void is exactly what you make of it. If you think of it as nothing, that's exactly what you get. If you think of it as a quaint flat on the upper east side of London," he looks around proudly, "that's what you get."

"Where's Murphy, Lucian?"

"That's a loaded question, isn't it?" He turns his back to me. "He's wherever he wants to be at the moment."

His words mimic Vita's. "You can't tell me you don't know where he is. You found me. Surely, you can find a hybrid."

He laughs. "You were easy to find. Let's just say you exude a very bright light." He turns, holding a plate with a sandwich. "Hungry?"

"Why are you stalling?"

He sets the plate on the table, sitting in the matching chair. "Stalling? What would I gain from stalling?" He takes a sip from his cup. "Oh, all right. You twisted my arm. I'll let you in on my secret. Mother should be here any minute." He smiles. "We can finally end all this mess, and I can be free of this world, once and for all."

"Killing me is still the plan?"

"Of course. I kill you, gain your powers, then she'll kill me and gain it all." He closes his eyes at the thought. "The promise of death is something I've treasured for centuries."

"Why would you want to die, Lucian?"

He takes a deep nasally breath. "It's what I'm meant to do. This is the entire reason for my existence." He sips from the edge of the cup. "You're the latest version of her plan to end them all. There have been many before you. I will give her credit, though. This has by far been my favorite. You have been very—entertaining."

"What about Shu?"

"What about him?" He bites a piece of something I can't see, chewing loudly.

"As long as he's still alive, neither you nor Vita will hold the full power of air."

He sighs deeply. "That's not my concern."

I focus my energy on my surroundings. In my mind, I imagine the void transforming into the small library hidden at Grimsgil. The void follows directions and manipulates itself into the quaint room. "What's this?" Lucian asks, looking around. "You changed our location." He claps his hands, slowly. "What a quick learner you are." The scene around me comes fully into view, and Lucian walks through the small room, running his fingers along the rows of ancient texts. "What a lovely library." He pulls out a large book and flips through the pages. "Why did you bring us here?"

Moving to an ancient scroll, still unrolled on the table,

"I wanted to show you something." He moves behind me, stepping over Murphy's vessel.

"What are we looking at?" he asks, following my finger across the page.

"Can you read Sanskrit?"

He moves closer to the script. "No, I'm afraid not. Reading has never been much of a priority for me."

"Do you know what these symbols mean?" He scoffs, stepping back.

"I had better things to worry about than human writings. What is the point of this?"

I point to a series of hieroglyphs scattered along the paper. I have absolutely no idea what they mean, but using the information he just shared, neither does Lucian. "They're about you," I lie.

He steps close again. "Me?" He smiles. "How exciting. What does it say?"

I pretend to read the pictures. "It's a little confusing. This one," I point at what looks like a palm branch. "This represents life." I pause for dramatic effect. "According to this, you were born to live a long fruitful life."

He makes an approving face. "Long, yes. Fruitful, maybe. Does it say anything else?" He looks over the top of my shoulder, clearly invested in my lies.

"Hmm," I fake concern. "It says you will inherit all power and..." I pause, pretending to be confused. "I'm not sure what this means."

"Well, don't stop now, girl. This is getting interesting."

"Dream walker. That's what it calls you, a dream walker." He takes a step backward.

"Dream walker," he echoes. "I like that. Although, I prefer the word nightmare. I invented that word, you know. Before me, there was no such thing as a nightmare." He smiles, proud of his revelation.

"Impressive," I agree, turning back toward the scroll. "It says you will inherit all power and become a dream walker. Wait..." I pause. "There's something else." He moves even closer, waiting for me to continue. "It talks about your parents."

"Parents? What does it say?"

I run my fingers along the pictures, continuing my facade. "He will be the son of aether and air and will have control over neither."

He wrinkles his forehead. "Aether and air? What does that mean?"

"Well, Vita was...is the Goddess of Aether, and Shu is the God of Air." I step away from the table, waiting for the dots to connect.

Lucian moves closer to the scroll, running his fingers along the pictures. "Shu? What does this mean?" He grabs the scroll off the table and pulls it apart. The ancient papyrus shreds in his hands.

"Oh, my gods. Do you think it means Shu is your father?" The library disappears, and I'm once again returned to the nothingness of the void. "Lucy?"

"Don't call me that." He appears in front of me in a flash of movement. "Maybe I won't wait on Mother to come. Maybe I'll just kill you now." He moves several feet in front of me. His energy has turned angry.

"Why do you think she wanted *me* to kill Shu?" I don't back down.

"Because she wants you to inherit his power. His, combined with yours, will give you full power."

"Not if there's more out there," I whisper. "If Shu's your father, you hold the power of air inside you. She wants *me* to kill Shu, gain his power, and then you kill me to gain the full power."

He covers his ears with his hands. "Shut up!"

"She didn't let you kill Shu because he's your father. Children of Firsts can kill a First, but she didn't want you to have to kill dear old Daddy."

Lucian slaps me across the cheek. "Shut up, bitch!"

"She's lied to you this whole time." I keep up the assault on his unstable mind. "Your father was right in front of you, and she denied you the knowledge."

"That's where I'm different from you. I don't need to know my father. I'm not human." He sends a blast of energy to the edge of the void, blowing a hole through the side. Through the hole, I see something that resembles moonlight.

"You're no different from me. We were both fathered by a god who didn't care about us. Left to fend for ourselves and survive the only way we know how. We're alike, you and I."

My words strike the chord I hoped they would. He sends another blast of energy, blowing a second hole in the void. On the other side, moonlight streams through.

"You can fix this." I pull Murphy to my side. "You can fix what she did."

Lucian turns toward me. "No, I'm done with you. Mother will come after you're dead and give me the honor of death." He lifts several feet off the ground.

"But Shu still lives," I remind him.

"He's not my concern!" he screams. "Your death *is* my concern."

"Think about it, Lucy. If you kill me before I kill Shu, you haven't completed the plan. He's still alive, carrying the power of air with him. You will have failed."

"Goodbye, bitch." I focus on the moonlight glistening through the hole, pulling myself and Murphy toward it. Whatever's on the other side will lead to death or freedom. That's better odds than I have here. Wrapping my arms around Murphy's vessel, I put every ounce of my energy into jumping us both to the moonlight, praying freedom awaits.

"No!" Lucian shouts from another place in time.

CHAPTER 17

$\mathscr{I}$t takes a few seconds for my eyes to adjust enough to realize I'm in a bedroom. Not any ordinary bedroom, wherever I am is lavishly and thoughtfully decorated. To my right is a large picture window and the source of the moonlight I saw from the void. In front of it sits a simple wooden desk with neatly stacked papers scattered along the corners. To my left, is a king-sized four-poster bed that backs up to a dark green wallpaper covered wall. The room is soft, beautiful, and comfortable. Where the hell am I?

A nightstand next to the bed is covered in pictures of a younger child. The pictures are from a time before modern photography. Several of them are carved into a piece of wood. Others are painted in different art styles. Behind me, a large fireplace covers most of the wall. It's not until I see the portrait hanging above it that I realize whose bedroom I'm in.

The woman in the portrait is slender, with a pointed

nose. Light brown hair is pulled high on her head, and she's dressed in what my best guess is Victorian-era clothing. The face of the woman who held me on the beach stares back at me, judging me for being in her room, and ultimately taking her life. "Well, hello, Vita."

I untie the sash and set Murphy's vessel on the edge of the bed. Whatever power Addy used to knock him out is effective. There have been no signs of movement from him since she worked her magic. I look around the room for any clues that might lead me to his soul. Something flashes from the edge of the desk. I stare blankly in the direction of the flash, trying to determine if what I saw was the product of an overly active imagination or real. The flash happens again, pulling my attention to a small piece of paper hidden between a stack of books. The paper looks as old as the scrolls from Grimsgil's library. I pull it from between two heavy books. Ancient writing covers the page, and it's in a language I don't recognize. Moonlight reflects off the writing, giving the words an otherworldly look. The words lift from the paper and float in front of my face.

"Welcome mín rís, how lothron mín n- -o service?" the letters dance in front of me before translating into a language I understand. *Welcome, my Queen, how may I be of service?*

My Queen? When Addy and I killed Vita, we inherited her power. Why did it take me this long to realize we're the Goddesses of Aether? That means this is our realm. I take a deep breath, relaxing my stance. "Show me where Murphy's soul is." The words barely leave my mouth before the scene around me changes. I'm standing in what looks like a prison cell, buried deep underground. His energy rushes me instantly.

"Murphy!" I yell through the vastness in front of me. No sound is returned. "Murphy!" I shout again, this time sending energy along with it. I can't pinpoint his location enough to jump to him, but I definitely feel the hint of his energy. Following the stone path further, the energy continues to grow. "Murphy!" I try again, focusing on moving both my energy and consciousness throughout the space. The stone that lines the walls appears more aged and worn the further I move. "Dammit! Where is he?"

On cue, the stone wall beside me rotates, opening a passageway that was hidden moments earlier. I don't question the movement and move through the newly opened passage. "Thank you," I whisper, rubbing my hands along the walls as I walk. The stone vibrates under my touch, responding to the feel of my movement against them. "Can you take me to Murphy?"

Ahead of me, the sound of ancient stones shifting and sliding echoes through the passage. The stone is showing me the way, transforming the maze as I go. Gaining confidence, I move faster through the newly created halls, and Murphy's energy continues to strengthen the further I go. "That's it, keep going," I whisper to the stone surrounding me. Following the scraping sounds, I move through the ancient passageway with complete trust in whatever supernatural force is leading the way.

The stone stops moving, emptying into a large room. "Light," I whisper. The room glows immediately, lit by an undetectable source. Allowing the energy to guide me, I follow, moving throughout the room. The energy pulls me to the back corner where I find what I've been searching for. Murphy, or at least something that looks like Murphy, is lying on a filthy cot. His body shimmers, and I can see the cot he's lying on through what's left of the rags he's wearing.

I try touching his shoulder, and my hand passes through the dense image. "Murphy?" I whisper, shaking the cot. "I'm here." Tears flood my eyes, looking at what's left of him. The strongest man I know is nothing more than a wisp of a soul. "Help me get him out of here," I say to whatever force guided me here. I try lifting him, and again my arms pass through his image.

"Gods, Murphy. I'm so sorry." Maybe I can put him inside the vessel and carry him that way. I turn, realizing the vessel is still in Vita's room. Shit! After all this, how the hell could I leave it behind?

Mira's words from when I first arrived in this realm come to mind. This realm is what I make of it. "Murphy, we're going to imagine our way out of here." I wrap a protective bubble of energy around Murphy's soul and attach it to mine. Closing my eyes, I envision Vita's chamber, where his empty vessel is peacefully resting. "Hang on," I whisper, as his soul and I are morphed out of the urine-filled dungeon and back into the lap of luxury.

I open my eyes and find the vessel in the same place I left it. Now I'm left with a new problem. How do I merge the two of them? Murphy's soul rests on the bed next to his vessel. "How do I do this?" I ask for help once more. With my words, a heavy book falls off the corner of the desk, opening magically to a page full of sigils and words in a language I don't understand. Pulling the book in my lap, I scan through the hieroglyphs, looking for something that might make sense. "I don't understand what you're trying to tell me. Help me," I whisper. The book transforms, and the pictures begin to move around, reshaping themselves on the page. They translate into a familiar language.

The soul and vessel should not be separated from each other. It is forbidden by The One, and only the combined powers of The One can repair what was wrongly separated.

I read over the highlighted words, not sure what they mean. Who or what is The One? If it was Vita, she's dead.

The book continues to vibrate in my hands, trying to tell me something. "I'm sorry, I don't understand."

Words form on the page in sequence, as if they're being written live. *"Help me, Goddess."*

I drop the book on the edge of the desk and move away. "Who are you?"

The cover of the book opens on its own as it begins to vibrate as the words form before my eyes. *"My name is Keegan Jacobson. Vita trapped me here."*

"Keegan? You're alive?"

"Trapped."

I pick the book up, "How do I free you?" The pages flip quickly toward the back of the book, and a smooth circle is drawn around a short passage.

"From the home that you were banished, to the realm where you are known, I release you from your binding and send you back home," I read the passage out loud.

The book falls from my hands as moonlight disappears from the window, replaced with bright streaks of lightning, flashing throughout the room. A man stands next to where the book landed. "Keegan?"

"Addy? You look different." His voice is hoarse, and his normally full beard is shaved clean.

"I'm not Addy, and you're not the Keegan I know." He stares at me with the same confused look I'm used to seeing. "I don't have time to explain. We have to get him out of here and get his soul back inside his vessel."

"Okay. How do we do that?"

"Weren't you just an all-knowing book? You should know how to do that."

Keegan laughs. "I was in the book, but I'm not all-knowing."

"Grab my arm. We have to get him to someone who will." I wrap Murphy's soul and vessel along with Keegan and me in a protective bubble, grab the translated book and imagine us traveling away from the void and back to the hallway where I left my new friends hours ago. Instantly, we're transported. Addy, Mira, Tempest, Peter, Mellan, and Kage are standing in front of me, staring at a closed door.

"Should we go after her?" Peter asks the group. "She just entered that hell, alone."

Keegan clears his throat. "Hi, guys."

Tempest turns, facing us. "Keegan?"

Keegan rushes the giant, hugging him tightly. "I missed you, man."

"How?" Kage asks, looking back at the door. "You closed the door less than a second ago and show up behind us with Jacobson and the soul."

"Time doesn't exist in the void," Mira answers. "When she returned to us, leaving the void behind, she chose to come back to this spot in time."

I shrug. "I don't understand it either." I pull the vessel and Murphy closer. "I have Murphy, but I don't know what to do next." Addy is the first to jump to our aid.

"How can we help?" I pull the translated book from under my arm, open it to the marked page, and hand it to her. She skims over the words. "What does this mean?"

"I was hoping one of you might understand."

Mira takes the book, saying the words out loud.

"No clue," Kage adds.

"Yeah, I've got nothing," Mellan says. "Keegan, you're the smart one. What do you think?"

"I don't know," he answers.

"Shit! Someone has to know."

"I believe that's my cue," a deep voice announces from behind us.

"Go away, Lucian," Addy says, taking the words out of my mouth. His boots echo off the wooden floor as he enters into the large hallway. The energy shifts as Kage and Mellan prepare to transform into their elemental forms.

"Oh, calm down, gentlemen. There's no need for all that." He smiles a wicked smile. "I'm here to offer my services."

"You don't offer anything without expecting something in return," Mira says, moving away from me and Addy.

"I could see how that could be misconstrued." His cane taps on the floor as he moves closer. "All I ask in return is to know who killed Mother." Addy and I look up in unison. "You can imagine my surprise when I found what was left of her body outside." He asks his question while staring at me.

"Your mother deserved to die," Kage says, distracting him. "She was a psychopath and a complete bitch." Mellan shoots Kage a warning look.

"She never claimed to be anything else," Lucian continues. "Now that she's dead, it seems that you need help to get him," he points to Murphy's soul, "inside of him." He points to the vessel.

"We don't need your help." Addy slides the book behind her slowly. Lucian moves closer to Murphy's soul and vessel. "Stay back," she warns.

Without warning, Lucian pounds his cane to the floor in a thunderous boom. The minute it hits, he disappears, taking the soul and vessel with him.

"No!" I shout. Addy and I grab hands, following the energy signature he left in his wake. We land on the cliffs outside, overlooking the pounding sea.

"Lucian, stop!" Addy shouts as we land a hundred yards in front of him. "We're going to follow you for as long as it takes. You're never going to escape us." Lucian smiles and disappears with a second boom. Like before, we follow, landing in the middle of the void.

"You two are stubborn, aren't you?" He pounds his cane a third time, and for the third time, we follow, landing on a small beach, where an old cabin barely held together with shards of wood sits.

"We're not going to stop," I repeat Addy's words from earlier.

"Lucian, that's enough." All three of us turn in the

direction of the voice. The cabin door opens, revealing a familiar figure, dressed in all white.

Lucian laughs. "Look what the cat dragged in." I watch as Shu saunters across the sand, toward where Lucian stands.

"I'm sorry," Shu says.

Lucian looks confused. "Why should I care about your feelings, Shu?"

"Because I left you alone with *her*, and I'm sorry." Lucian shifts from foot to foot.

"How dare you speak of Mother with that tone!" Lucian's body language has changed. "She was the greatest gift of all." Shu continues moving toward Lucian. Seeing them together, the similarities are obvious. Lucian has Shu's coloring, and they share the same eyes.

"I'm sorry for what she did to you, and I'm sorry I didn't stop it. "

"Seems you have that reputation," Addy mumbles.

"Stop!" Lucian shouts toward Shu. "I'll kill him," he points at Murphy's vessel and soul. "He's what she wants." He scowls in my direction. "You're here for her, not me. You've never been here for me." Lucian's words remind me of a hurt child.

"You're right, and I'm sorry for that. You should never have been born. Two gods aren't supposed to be able to produce an offspring."

"Not helping," Addy warns.

"Surprise, Father. Here I am. What do you think of this abomination you created?" He bends down, touching Murphy's vessel.

"I think you're nothing more than a scared and lonely

little boy who looks for friends by haunting human nightmares." Shu continues to move toward Lucian. "I'm here now. Let me make up for the time I missed with you."

"Do you think this is an episode of Dr. Phil?" Lucian asks. How the hell does he know who Dr. Phil is? "One cannot simply make up for centuries with simple words. I do believe you've been in the human world for far too long." He sends a blast of energy into Murphy's vessel, making it shake on impact.

"No!" I move closer to Lucian. "Leave him alone."

Lucian turns to me. "Or what?" He sends another blast of energy, making the vessel shake uncontrollably.

"Or I'll kill you." Lucian laughs at my warning.

"You can't kill me." He sends a blast of energy, this time straight into Addy. It hits her dead center, throwing her back to the edge of the shore. She's unconscious and lying in a heap on the sand. "Weaklings, all of you."

"Your mother didn't think we were weak when we killed her!" My words anger him. His body begins shaking.

Shu makes eye contact with me as his words echo through my mind. "*Only the combined powers of The One. Get the other Adria, now!*" I jump to Addy, pulling her up from the sand. She coughs before opening her eyes, looking around for clues.

"You good?" she nods, standing to her feet. "We have to combine our powers to defeat him. Like we did for Vita." Addy grabs my hand and together we face the monster that is Lucian. Shu vanishes from his side of the beach, appearing next to me. He grabs my free hand, making me the center conduit for both of their powers.

"Now," he whispers, and I release the power building inside of me from our connection.

Lucian smiles as the power flows into him. "Finally!" he says, lifting off of the ground. White light flows from his eyes, his hands, and his feet. The scene reminds me of something out of a horror movie. His mouth opens, spewing the light into the world. "I'm coming, Mother." He doesn't try to fight as his words are nothing more than a cry. The light fades, and he falls to the sand with a lifeless thud.

The three of us stand in silence as the reality of the situation crashes down. Murphy! I run to the vessel and soul, who despite being tortured by Lucian are both alive. "Shu? What do I do?"

Shu bows to one knee in front of Addy and me. "You are The One. Together, you are the combined power of one. Use that power to put him together and take him home."

Addy takes my hand into hers as we kneel side by side. I place a free hand near Murphy's soul while Addy places hers on his vessel. Without words, we close our eyes in unison. The power flowing through our connection is unmeasurable. I feel the instant his soul joins the vessel. What was separate is now joined as one. I open my eyes to see familiar blue eyes staring back at me.

"Murphy?" His eyes close as quickly as they opened. His soul is inside this vessel, I can feel it.

"He's weak, but he's whole," Shu says, moving beside us. Addy stands, moving away from Shu. He steps in front of her, blocking her movement.

"What the hell are you doing?" Her words are laced with venom. "Get away from me."

"I'm doing what I should've done earlier. I'm apologizing." He lowers his head.

"I think you're confused about how to apologize," Addy spits.

"Addy, stop." I move to her side. "He's here, and without him, we couldn't have killed Lucian."

She looks into the sky. "Where is he? Where's my Shu? Where's his apology?" Her words echo through the emptiness.

"I don't know where he is, but I'm here for both of you," Shu answers.

She transforms into pure energy and lifts off of the beach. "Addy?" I yell after her.

"She's hurt," Shu answers. "Give her some time." He turns toward me. "Adria, I'm so sorry for all the pain I caused. My arrogance led to all of this." He pauses. "I hurt you. I hurt Claire. I hurt Lucian." He turns toward the carcass of his son. "I'm the one responsible for his pain and the pain he's caused humans over the years."

"You don't get to take ownership of everything that's plagued our world." I move back to Murphy's side. "You're not the priority right now. I have to get him back to our realm. We'll deal with all of this later."

He nods. "We have to take him back to the castle. That's where the portal is."

"Portal?"

"How do you think I got here?" I roll my eyes not sure I care at the moment. "Touch his shoulder and take us to the castle." I wrinkle my forehead at him. "Adria, you're the Goddess of Aether. This is your realm. All you have to do is think it, and it will happen." He takes my hand into his.

I close my eyes, picturing Vita's castle. When I open them, we're surrounded by three balls of energy, a wall of water, a roaring tornado, and a confused hybrid, standing outside of the castle.

CHAPTER 18

"*A*dria?" Tempest says, transforming back to human form. "Where's Addy?" he looks behind me for his mate.

"I don't know," I answer truthfully. "She's alive but needed some time to think. We need to get Murphy to the portal."

"There's a portal?" Mira asks, turning back into her familiar form. I lift Murphy's body using air and follow Shu inside the castle with a crew lagging behind.

Shu leads us down the same passage we traveled earlier. "Why are we going back to the void?"

"The void is whatever we want it to be. For you, it was a place where you were lost and confused. For Vita and Lucian, it was a place they could control and turn into anything they wanted. For me, it's a passageway from realm to realm." We stop at the blank door from earlier. Shu turns toward my new friends. "You cannot enter this room. You will not return if you do."

Mellan steps forward. "I don't know how things run in your realm, but in this one, we do as we please." He moves closer to the door.

"In my realm, you don't exist." Shu's words are harsh. "Or if you do, you're nothing more than an average, run-of-the-mill human, who works nine to five, making money for someone else."

"Seems you're a bastard in every realm," Mellan retorts.

"Maybe I am, but this bastard is saving your life." He turns to me. "Adria, bring him inside." I turn to my new friends.

"When we killed Vita, Addy and I inherited her power. We share the element of aether now."

"No wonder she needed time to think," Peter responds.

"We'll be here when she's ready." Mira gives me a quick hug. "I'll see you in your dreams," she whispers in my ear. I smile, hugging her back.

"Tempest?" He looks up at his name. "Will you tell Addy goodbye for me?" He nods without words.

"Thank you for freeing me." Keegan gives me a quick hug.

"Ready?" I turn toward Shu.

"As I'll ever be," he answers, grabbing my hand and opening the door. The three of us are enveloped in the familiar blackness. "Pull Murphy close to you." I follow directions, and he wraps his arms around both of us. "Take us home, my dear."

"Me? You're the one who passes through realms in here."

"True, but you're the one that's strong enough to get all three of us to the same realm at the same point in time." He smiles like this is something I know how to do.

"Seriously?"

"Seriously. Just think about where you want us to go, and we'll go. How many times do I have to tell you how powerful you are?"

I sigh deeply before closing my eyes. I picture the office turned into a hospital room at the fire castle. My entire body emits a low vibration before being suddenly pulled through what feels like reaching the top peak of a roller-coaster, just before the chains release. Movement stops, and I open my eyes. Shu still has his arms wrapped around Murphy and me and boasts a smug look on his face. I roll my eyes, making sure he can see.

"Adria, Murphy?" Bonnie's familiar voice calls from across the room. Tempest is the first to our side, picking up Murphy and moving him to a bed along the wall. Bonnie rushes to his side as Ethan, Sophie, and Keegan rush into the room.

Keegan moves to my side. "Are you all right?" He looks me over, head to toe, for any obvious injuries.

I nod. "I'm fine."

"What happened?" he asks as Shu moves closer to his favorite place in my castle, the brandy cart. "How did he... I mean." He looks between the two of us. "Hello, Shu." Keegan waves as Shu pours a glass of brandy. Shu waves back using his middle finger while his hand is wrapped around the glass of dark liquid. Keegan's eyes grow wide with questions.

"We have much to talk about." I smile.

"That's an understatement," he whispers as he joins the small group crowded around Murphy.

Brenna moves to my side. "You did it." She hugs me tightly before dropping to both knees and lowering her head. "My Queen."

"There'll be none of that, Brenna. You haven't bowed to anyone for centuries. I don't expect you to start doing it now." I help her to her feet.

Rhys and Stephen enter the room. They're wearing matching green jackets. When they see the chaos in front of them, they rush to my side. Both men give me a heart-felt hug, and I return it with love. "Thank you, both."

"He's awake!" Bonnie says with a clap. I move to Murphy's side. He smiles a crooked grin when he sees me, two dimples showing on the sides of his cheeks.

"Hey," his voice is raspy and sounds nothing like Murphy.

"Hey, yourself." He slowly moves his hand off his chest, reaching for mine. I meet him halfway, lacing my fingers through his. His eyelids look heavy, as he struggles to keep them open. "Get some rest. You're safe."

He smiles, and his eyes close completely. Bonnie looks at the lifeless Murphy vessel on the gurney on the other side of the room. "What about him?" she asks, pointing at the second vessel.

"Can we do anything to make him more comfortable?" I step beside the empty vessel. Deep black bruises cover the tops of his sunken cheeks. This body looks so small, so fragile. It's nothing more than skin and bone. Each rib is visible through the thin sheet that covers him. Even his thick, red curls are darker and thinned out. This body is lifeless and will never be capable of sustaining life again.

Bonnie steps beside me, taking my hand in hers. "This body will be gone within the day. I'm surprised he's held on for this long." I nod, understanding. "We'll pay our respects when he passes. It shouldn't be long."

Shu toasts the air in front of him at her words. "It's a plan."

"You're being even more of an asshole than usual."

"You're welcome." He smiles, handing me a matching glass to his. "We need to talk."

"Later." I walk away from my grandfather. Shu appears in front of me, stopping my escape.

"I believe now is the best choice, Your Highness." His smile doesn't reach his dark eyes.

"It's all right, dear. I'll let you know if anything changes with Murphy." Bonnie stands vigil at her son's side.

I motion in front of me. "After you." Shu leads us from the study, across the grand hallway onto the back veranda. He closes the door behind us, leading me even further away from the castle.

"Where are we going?"

"Away from Brenna's nosey ears." He moves to the furthest point on the balcony from the castle before motioning to an empty chaise beside him. "Adria, I'm sorry." He sighs before continuing. "This isn't easy for me, so don't interrupt, or I'll get sidetracked." I smile at his admission. "I'm sorry for lying to you. But please know, everything I did, I did with you in mind."

Hearing his admission doesn't ease the tension

between the two of us. "That doesn't make everything okay."

"Don't interrupt," he reminds me. I open my eyes wide, encouraging him to continue. "I've lied to you about many things. The first was Lucian." Shu stands, moving toward the edge. "Vita never told me she was pregnant, but when I heard rumors of her child's existence...I feared he was mine." He somehow produces a glass of brandy I didn't notice in his hands, drinking half of it in one gulp. "She did unspeakable things to him. She brainwashed him, all in the name of love. I could have saved him. I *should've* saved him."

I stand, moving closer to my grandfather. "I'm sorry, Shu. I can't imagine what it would be like to watch your child die in front of you. Whether you raised him or not, he was still your son. I wish it could've ended differently."

"Me too." His voice is full of emotion. "There was no other way."

"That's why you went to that realm? That's why you were with Vita, in her castle?"

Shu takes another drink. "Yes. I had to try and save him. Even if it was a few millennia too late."

"I'm sorry you weren't able to succeed, but I don't accept your apology. Do you know how alone I felt?" Anger replaces the compassion I felt moments earlier. "Do you know what it felt like think you had been with her the whole time?" My words sound selfish, and I don't care. I send a shock wave into Shu, making him drop his drink. "Do you want to know what the worst part was?"

Shu straightens his white suit jacket, wiping an invisible stain from the front. "I'm sure you're going to tell me."

"Damn straight, I'm going to tell you." I stand, moving closer. "The worst part was thinking that I could trust you. Thinking that you were sorry for keeping me hidden from Llyr my whole life. Thinking you were trying to make it up to me. Thinking that you...that you loved me." My voice cracks with my words. "Only to realize that I was on my own, yet again."

"You weren't on your own, Adria. You had the seventh realm elementals, and you had me. I was working from inside the castle."

"How the hell was I supposed to know that? For all I knew, you were fucking Vita and didn't give a shit about anyone else. That's certainly how it came across to me." I send another shock wave to him, frizzing out his hair.

He holds his hands flat in front of him, surrender style. "I can assure you I wasn't," he pauses, "fucking anyone." He physically shivers at the thought. "I was there for you. I was there for Lucian. I was there for redemption."

"Redemption?" I question. "It's going to take a lot more than that for redemption."

"I know." His words are softer, and he's lost the usual air of royalty he carries with him. "I'm truly sorry, Adria. I do love you." I turn my back to him, heading back inside. "Adria?" Against my better judgment, I turn back. "I'm married," he pauses. "His name is Tucker, and we share the most glorious bungalow on my island off the coast of France."

My mind flashes back to Tucker and the solitude of his life. "I know," I answer. "We met."

"Ask me anything." Shu steps toward me. "I will never lie to you again."

"Why?"

Shu looks puzzled. "Why what?"

"Why did Llyr have to die while you got to live?" I turn, walking back into the castle. I don't need to see his face to know how badly my words hurt him. For a moment, I feel guilty and fight the urge to apologize. His energy rushes me. It's filled with loneliness and sadness. I feel him jump from the castle, leaving me to deal with my anger alone.

"There's been no change," Bonnie says as I enter the room. She nods toward the empty vessel. "For either of them."

"Are you okay?" Tempest asks, coming to my side. "That seemed like it was going to be intense."

"Intense, it was." I smile a fake smile. "Do you know that in the seventh realm, you and Addy are an item?"

"Addy?"

"Seventh realm version of Adria. She's kind of a hard pill to swallow, but she's tough as nails." Tempest is at a loss for words. He stares at me, unsure what to say, making me laugh for the first time in a while. "Don't worry. You're safe." I pat him on the shoulder.

"Was I there? In the seventh realm?" Keegan asks, moving toward us.

"You were. I found you trapped in the void."

His eyes widen. "Seriously? Did you free that version of me, or is he still trapped?"

"I freed him and before you ask, no, I don't know why Vita trapped him. He was trapped inside an ancient book in Vita's bedroom."

Keegan smiles. "That leaves me with so many questions."

I laugh. "Yeah, you and me both."

"That version of you must be an asshole, too." Tempest pats his friend on the back.

"Adria!" Bonnie calls from across the room. "He's awake again." All three of us rush to his side.

"You're an asshole in every realm," Murphy whispers at Keegan, followed by a smile.

"I may be, but gods, it's good to see you talking again." He takes Murphy's hand and brings it to his chest. "You look good, man."

Murphy turns to Tempest. "Thank you, both. I don't know everything that's happened, but I know you were both at my side."

"They were. In every realm," I confirm.

"I love you," he mouths to me. His words have faded to nothing more than air.

"I love you, too." I manage to get the words out before tears fall.

"Lucian? Vita?" he whispers.

"Gone," I answer, stroking his red curls. "They're both gone."

"Are you?" I nod, knowing what his question is. "Your Highness," he whispers. His eyelids start to droop.

"Get some rest. We'll be here." He nods, letting his eyelids fall completely closed.

"Poor baby. He's exhausted," Bonnie says, covering

Murphy only the way a mother can. She tucks the sheet tightly around his body, making him resemble a giant burrito.

To my right, the sound of someone gasping for air grabs our attention. The empty vessel is sucking in deep breaths, trying to get air into the tired and sick body. "Oh, dear," Bonnie says, moving to the vessel. "I'm afraid it's time." Everyone in the room gathers around the vessel that once looked like the man I love and now resembles nothing more than a shell of a human. Bones, covered by skin, are all that remains of the once virile man.

"Thank you for living as long as you could." My words carry through the room as I send a blast of love and gratitude into the vessel. He releases a deep breath, and the body relaxes completely.

"He's gone," Brenna announces.

CHAPTER 19

The next week is nothing more than a blur. Murphy continues to improve. Bonnie and Sophie refuse any magical help as they struggle to get him up the stairs and into his room several times each day. "We humans aren't completely helpless," Bonnie keeps reminding me as the three of them make their way slowly up the stairs. I do manage to sneak a small bit of air element into their climb when they're not paying attention, lifting Murphy's weight off the two of them and his wobbly legs.

Instead of sleeping in my bedroom suite, I've spent each night and most days in his, watching his hybrid body heal. With his soul intact, his body is healing at a supernatural pace. His mind, on the other hand, is not.

Most of his days and nights are spent sleeping. Over the span of a twenty-four-hour day, Murphy sleeps at least twenty of them. Tempest and Keegan have both assured me it's normal and necessary for elemental healing. The nights are the worst. Every night since returning, his sleep is filled with dreams and nightmares that I don't know how to fix. His body twitching so much, he wakes me from my restless sleep. Tonight is no different.

"Murphy?" He doesn't answer. His eyes are moving so quickly under his eyelids, I can only imagine what he's experiencing isn't pleasant. Holy shit. I'm the Goddess of Aether. I don't have to imagine. Why the hell did it take me this long to figure that out?

I lace my fingers through his, turning my body to face him. His fingers are clinching open and closed as I hold on, focusing myself on the moment and into the world he's facing right now. "I'm coming, Murphy," I whisper, just as I'm swept away into what I assume is the void.

The darkness transforms into the prison cell Shu and I found in the tunnels of Petra. Murphy's in the far corner, covered in dirt. His body is weak and shivering from the cold. To my right, the stack of rat carcasses lies covered in buzzing flies and maggots. "Murphy?" I lean down, touching his head.

"Adria?" He looks up quickly. "How are you here?" He struggles to stand. "Have I gone mad?" He looks around, seeing the closed door behind me.

"You can see me?" I ask, surprised.

Tears stream down his cheeks. "Yes." He stumbles, catching himself on the wall. "Is this a dream?" He looks around the room again for a clue as to what's going on.

"I don't know. Maybe?" I touch his shoulder. His body is thin with neglect. "You're safe."

"I don't like this dream." He falls to one knee, barely able to hold his weight. A shuffling sound echoes through the hallway, crescendoing, as it moves closer to his room. "Shit," he whispers. "You need to hide."

"What is that?"

"It's a who." He falls back to the floor. "I don't know if I'm dreaming, or if she'll be able to see you, but I don't want to take any chances." I slide into the shadows of the room as the steel door to Murphy's prison rattles open.

"Good morning," a shaky voice announces. I instantly recognize her energy. She's the same one who was bringing Brenna food when I rescued her. "Oh, dear." She scuffles toward a bowl on the ground. "You didn't eat." She scoots closer to Murphy and my hiding spot. "You need to eat. You must keep your strength up."

"I can't eat that shit," Murphy mumbles. "It's rat food."

"I'm sorry. It's all I have." She steps into the light, allowing me to see her for the first time. She's no taller than a child, but from what I can tell, it's not because she's short. She's stooped over, nearly bent in half from a crooked back. Her skin is faded blue and what hair she has left is clumped over her scalp in tiny patches. She's wearing a cloak and resembles something from nightmares. "She's going to take you away."

Murphy looks up. "Away?"

"To another island. They're preparing to leave now."

"I hope it's as nice as this one. It's going to be hard to beat this five-star resort." Despite his condition and surroundings, Murphy still has a sense of humor.

"It will make this one look like the Ritz Carlton," the old woman answers. "You have to stay strong." She moves to a wall behind him, scratching something into the wall.

"I can't decide if you're trying to kill me or help me."

The woman steps within inches of Murphy. "All I've ever wanted was to help you." In an instant, the scene disappears, and we're swept into another room. This one is even darker and smellier than the last.

"Murphy!" I shout, seeing him slumped in a small heap in the corner of the cell. He's smaller and so dirty, I can barely make out his features. This is the room I found him in. Or at least what I thought was him. All I found was an empty vessel.

I shake his shoulders, trying to rouse him from sleep. It's no use. He's lifeless. I fight tears threatening to fall. "He's gone," a familiar voice says from across the room. I turn to see the woman from earlier. She shuffles her way toward me, barely able to move.

"Stop," I warn. "Who are you?"

The woman laughs. "That's a good question. I know who I once was. Now, I don't know." I study her features. Her eyes are faded with age but show evidence of the beauty that once hid behind them. Wrinkled blue skin is dry and hangs loosely on her face. Her cheeks are sunken from malnourishment.

"Who *were* you?" I'm not sure I want the answer.

She attempts to smile. "My name was Mared, and I was once very beautiful." She closes her eyes at a memory. Her eyes open as she attempts to lower herself onto one knee. "Your father was my God, as you are now my Goddess."

"You're a water elemental?"

"Aye," she whispers. "I was a siren."

"What happened to you?"

She struggles back to her feet. "I was captured and thrown into the void by Vita."

"Vita? Why would she capture you?" I realize how straight forward my words sounded. "I'm sorry. I don't mean to be rude."

"No offense taken." She leans against the wall for support. "It's a very good question. There are hundreds of sirens out there, why choose me for this life of glamor?" She coughs out a laugh. "It took me twenty-five years to figure it out myself." She looks down at Murphy's weakened vessel. "Because of him."

I follow her line of sight. "What did Murphy have to do with you becoming captive to Vita?"

"He's my son." Instantly, I'm drawn out of the dream and back into the bed beside Murphy. His eyes open at the same time mine do.

"What?" he says, smiling at me.

"Were you dreaming?" His smile fades, and he rolls away from me.

"Just more of the same." He sighs. "I keep returning to places I'd rather forget."

I slide out of bed. "Are you hungry? I'm sure Rhys or Stephen or Bonnie have food waiting on you."

"Yes, starved," he answers. He stops and stares at me. "This is the first time I've felt hungry." He slowly works his way out of bed, taking a minute to stand to full height. "I could use a shower."

He looks healthier than before. "I'll go get something to eat while you shower. Will you be okay in there alone?" He wiggles his eyebrows, reminding me of the old Murphy.

"I'll manage." I kiss him on the cheek before taking his arm into mine and leading him to the bathroom. "Adria, I'm okay to do this on my own. I seriously feel better."

"Okay." I step away, watching him walk. He's right, he's more stable than I've seen him and looks physically stronger. I wait until he's safely in the bathroom before leaving.

Downstairs, the hospital room has been cleared and the room returned to my office. Bonnie is the first to greet me. She and Ethan are sitting on the couch while Ethan pours over the ancient texts Brigit stored in this library.

"Good afternoon!" she says joyfully. "How is he today?"

"He's much better. He's in the shower and asked for something to eat."

Her eyebrows raise. "Are you sure it's safe for him to be in there alone?"

"I'm not going to leave him long. I just came down for some food." Bonnie jumps to her feet.

"Let me find something." I follow her into the kitchen. Stephen and Rhys have a smorgasbord of goodies set on the counter. "It's called a charcuterie board." Bonnie sweeps her hand across the spread of cheese, fruit, and meat. With her accent, it sounds like she's telling me it's some sort of coochie board, but I don't question her. She gathers a small sample of each item onto a plate and grabs a bottle of water from the cabinet. "Maybe he'll feel like coming downstairs after his shower?" she asks, handing me the plate of food.

"I'll ask." I smile, turning back toward the stairs. "Bonnie?"

"Yes, dear?"

"Do you know anything about Murphy's biological mother, the elemental?"

She sighs. "No. Only that I'm grateful to her for leaving him with Llyr. Why do you ask?"

I shrug. "No reason." I head upstairs, balancing the food carefully. Murphy's already out of the shower and lying on the bed. He's wearing a pair of gray sweatpants and is shirtless. His red curls are wet and clinging tightly to his head.

"You survived the shower?"

"It was touch and go there for a minute, but I persevered. I feel like a new man." He sits up, scooting to the back of the headboard. "Is that for me?" He's staring at the plate of food Bonnie sent.

"Yes, it's some sort of coochie."

He laughs. "I'm so hungry, I don't care whose coochie it is." He takes the plate and begins devouring the food. "I did have a strange dream." He slows down long enough to announce.

I wrinkle my forehead at him. "What?"

"You asked if I was dreaming last night." He shoves a piece of square cheese in his mouth. "I dreamed you were there with me."

"There with you?"

"In the cell." He eats a piece of pepperoni. "The first place where they held me. I don't remember you being there, but in my dream, you were."

I sit on the edge of the bed. "I went into your dream while you were sleeping."

He stops chewing. "You did?"

"I could tell you were having a dream, and I went in to see if I could help. I'm sorry. I realize now that I completely invaded your space. That was wrong of me and makes me no better than Lucian."

"I'm not mad," he says, setting his plate on the table next to the bed. "Whatever happened in that dream helped me. I feel stronger today. For the first time that I can remember, I feel like myself. Did anything happen while you were there? Did you change something?"

I shake my head. "No. I was just there, watching." I sigh, not sure how much I need to tell him. "The dream started in Petra at the cell you were in first. Then transported to an island off of Greece."

"I don't remember that island."

"You were pretty much gone by that time." He lays his head on the tall headboard.

"Gone? You mean my soul was not with my body."

"Yea. There's something else." He pulls his head up. "Do you remember meeting someone while you were being held prisoner?"

He waits a minute before answering. "Maybe? It feels like I did, but I can't quite put a finger on who or what. Did you see someone?" His eyes close slightly. "I think the shower and a full stomach wore me out." He burps loudly, opening his eyes wide with embarrassment. "Excuse me."

"Get some rest. I'll be here when you wake."

He nods. "If I have another nightmare, come into the dream. It's not invading if you have permission." He scoots back under the covers, fluffing his pillow underneath him.

"I'm going to take this downstairs and talk to Ethan.

I'll be back." My words are lost as Murphy floats back to sleep and away from our conversation.

Ethan's still on the couch, pouring through stacks of ancient books. His ability to read and comprehend this amount of knowledge astounds me. Moving a few books from the empty seat beside him, I sit. "Find anything interesting?"

Ethan, who just noticed anyone was in the room with him, looks up startled. "Adria!" He smiles. "These books are filled with information never seen before. Thank you for allowing me access to them."

"Anytime." I return the smile. "Do you mind if I ask you a few questions?"

He closes the encyclopedia-looking book he's holding, giving me his full attention. "Of course, dear. I'll do my best to answer."

"It's about Murphy. Well, about his mother, really."

Ethan looks around the room. "Where is Bonnie?"

"Not Bonnie. His birth mother."

His eyebrows raise with understanding. "The water elemental?"

"Do you know anything about her?" He stands, putting his hand on my shoulder.

"It's best we go outside." I follow him to the veranda and watch as Ethan closes the door behind us. "I don't want Bonnie to hear us talking." I nod, sitting beside him on a long swing. "Llyr told me about her."

"Llyr knew his mother?"

"Aye, she was a siren. Llyr told me she was captured. He never said by who or what, just that she was captured and wouldn't be able to raise Murphy."

"I thought Murphy was left on Llyr's doorstep?"

"That's what Llyr told us at first. He later admitted the truth."

"Did he say anything about her? About his mother?"

He sighs. "Not much really. Just that she was captured and left behind a baby that needed parents."

"Did he ever say her name or what she looked like?"

Ethan searches for a lost memory. "He never said what she looked like, but I would imagine she would've had blue-green skin like all sirens do when in elemental form." He pauses. "I think her name started with an M. Mary or Marner or..."

"Mared?" I interrupt.

"Yes! That's it. Mared. How'd you know that?"

"I think she's the reason Murphy survived as long as he did. I think Vita was the one who captured her, and in true Vita fashion, she made sure they were together in captivity."

CHAPTER 20

I've been lying beside Murphy for a few hours. He's sleeping soundly without any trace of nightmares or obvious reason for me to invade his dreams. My thoughts keep flashing back to Mared and how misshapen her body was. How could a water elemental age like that? She looked more like an elderly witch than a beautiful siren. I jump to the library and beside Ethan again.

"Goodness! You frightened me." He drops his latest book in his lap.

"I didn't mean to scare you," I apologize. "I have another question."

"Okay." He turns, facing me completely. "I'll do my best to answer."

I sigh, trying to find the right words. "In all of your readings and discoveries, have you found any information on what would happen to an elemental if they were completely isolated from their element?"

"Hmm," he moans. "Like a fire elemental being surrounded by water, or an air elemental forced into a cage?"

"Or a water elemental denied access to water," I add. Ethan stands, stepping toward a bookshelf on the opposite wall. He pulls out an ancient text, smaller than its surrounding neighbors. "Here." He points at a passage and reads. "If a lesser is taken away from their element for an extended time, they will lose their ability to control their element. Rapid aging, depression, and dementia are just a few of the possible effects of the separation." He looks up. "Does that answer your question?"

"I think it might. Thank you." I jump back to bed and beside Murphy. His eyes are moving quickly, and his body is shaking. "Murphy?" I whisper. He doesn't respond. I pull myself as close to him as possible. Closing my eyes, I'm instantly transported to the void and the cell on the island in Greece. His body is lying in the same place as before. It's lifeless and sickly looking.

"You're back," Mared says from across the room.

"I am. I came to see you."

"Me?" she asks with surprise. "What do I owe this honor?" Her feet slowly shuffle their way across the stones as she moves closer.

"Does he know who you are?"

Her voice cracks when she speaks. "No. I wouldn't burden him with that."

"You're the reason he stayed alive?"

She moves to his side. "I sent him away."

"What do you mean?"

"I sent his soul away."

"You did what?" I ask, not sure I heard correctly.

"I sent his soul away," she repeats. "I sent him somewhere she couldn't find him. Someplace I created. I couldn't stand to watch him suffer." For once in her life, Vita had been telling me the truth. She really didn't know where he was. Shit.

"How? How did you have the power to do that?"

Mared laughs a deep, raspy laugh. "I've lived down here long enough to pick up a few things." A cough follows her laugh. "Truthfully, it took every bit of strength I had left." She turns to Murphy. "I'd do it all again if I had the chance. His soul is free of this torture."

"It was the second time you'd saved him, wasn't it?" She smiles. "You left him at Llyr's when he was a baby."

Mared looks down. "I didn't have a choice. I knew Llyr was the only one who could protect him. He deserved a safe home where he could grow and become what he was meant to be."

"Why?"

"Vita," she answers simply. "She was appearing in my dreams, and I knew it was only a matter of time before she would get him."

I look at the empty vessel huddled next to us. "Why would she want to hurt him?"

Mared sighs, moving slowly toward the wall to lean on it. "You," she answers simply. "She wanted to hurt you."

"That makes no sense. I wasn't even born yet."

"She's wanted to hurt you since before your conception. Your birth was prophesied. I don't know how she discovered he would be a part of your life, but she did and wanted him dead. I didn't have a choice and didn't know what else to do." Mared pauses. "When she learned what I'd done, she brought me here." She rubs her hands along her tattered robes.

"I can help you." My words are no louder than a whisper.

She scoffs. "I'm beyond help, my dear. I'm one step away from death. Protecting Murphy was my last hoorah." Her timbre matches mine.

"You're not beyond my help. A lesser elemental cannot be removed from their element. It causes them to dwindle and age. I can get you out of here."

She pauses, looking at the crumpled body of her son. "I won't leave him. Not again."

"What's left in this cell is nothing more than an empty vessel. Murphy's with me, and he's whole. I found his soul and returned it to a healthier vessel."

"You found his soul? How?"

"It's a long story." I smile.

Mared stares blankly at me. "What about the woman?"

"She's at the same place as Murphy."

"Will you take me to him?" her voice cracks with emotion.

"I will." I step closer to her. "May I heal you first?"

She wipes a stray tear. "Yes." I lay a hand on each of her shoulders and close my eyes. I envision the water, bringing new life into her tired, neglected body. I pull on the love for her son and send it to her, making her cleansed and whole.

Mared transforms before my eyes. Her weakened, bent body slowly rises, bringing her eyes level with mine. Loose, sagging skin tightens, closing the gaps between her skull and the bags previously hanging from it. Dark red hair fills in the top of her head where only white patches were before.

Bent, crooked hands form into perfectly shaped fingers, and small gills form at the base of her neck. The woman standing in front of me looks to be the same age as me. She smiles, showing a snow-white smile, and wipes the tears streaming down her cheeks. She bows, prostrate to the floor, with ease. "Your Highness, I am forever in your favor."

"Please stand. You owe me nothing." She follows orders, standing back to full height. "I've restored what was wrongfully taken from you."

She wraps her arms around me. "Thank you doesn't seem adequate. I've forgotten what it feels like to be... normal. How can I repay you?"

"Live your life, and be happy. That's how you can repay me." She steps away, still wiping tears, and nods. "Are you ready to see your son?"

Mared nods and closes her eyes. "Yes, but I don't want him to know who I am. He has a mother. One who raised him and loves him as much as I do. I don't want to make that confusing."

"I understand." I reach for her hand. "But I can't keep your secret. Murphy deserves to know you as much as you deserve to know him." So much of my life has been spent in lies, I won't perpetuate that by keeping this secret. "You're right. Murphy has a wonderful mother who has raised him to be the remarkable man he is. Trust me when I say he has enough love for both of you."

Mared wipes a stray tear at my words and nods. "Thank you." She squeezes my hand. "I'm ready."

I jump the two of us to the courtyard of the fire castle. The sun is beginning to set, casting its usual eerie glow over the open land. Mared takes a deep breath before following me through the front door.

Bonnie and Sophie are alone in the large foyer, rear-ranging furniture. "Adria!" Sophie says as we enter. "I hope you don't mind. We're moving a few things around. This place just seems so..."

"Red?" I complete her sentence.

"That's the perfect description. We thought if we arranged some of the larger pieces of furniture, it might break up the monotony of the color palette."

"You have my permission to move whatever you want."

"Oh, hello?" Bonnie says, moving toward Mared. "I didn't see you there."

"Bonnie. This is Mared. Vita was holding her captive. I helped her escape." I turn toward the siren beside me. "Mared. These two lovely ladies are Bonnie and Sophie. Murphy's mother and sister."

"You know Murphy?" Sophie asks.

"Aye...we were held captive together," Mared answers with a smile.

Bonnie steps in front of the tall woman and wraps her short arms around her waist. "Bless you, dear. I can't imagine what you went through. Are you hungry?"

"Who are you trying to feed now, Mom?" Murphy asks, walking into the foyer. His eyes are bright, and he looks more like himself than earlier.

"Oh, you know me. I feed everyone," Bonnie answers with a laugh. "It's my love language."

"Do I know you?" he asks the woman standing next to me.

Mared turns toward me, not sure what to say. I take a deep breath before answering for her. "Mared has something she would like to tell you, privately."

Murphy smiles warmly. "If it's alright with you, Mared, you can tell me here. I don't keep secrets from my family."

Mared nods. "I understand." She wraps her fingers through mine, holding tight. "We were both held captive by Vita."

Murphy wrinkles his forehead, trying to remember. "I'm sorry. I don't remember much from that time."

"That's a blessing, isn't it? I looked a bit different when I was there." She turns toward me. "Adria restored my health."

"She has a way of doing that." Murphy moves to my side and kisses me on the top of my head.

"Nearly twenty-six years ago I left my hybrid son with Llyr, my God." Mared's voice is shaky as she admits the secret she's held for a quarter of a century.

Murphy stares at the beautiful siren. "What does that mean?"

"It means Mared is your mother," Bonnie says, stepping in front of the siren. She wraps her short arms around her waist and pulls her close. "Thank you. I can't imagine making a decision like that. I know it wasn't easy."

"You're my birth mother?" Murphy asks, putting the pieces together in slow motion.

"Aye," Mared whispers.

"I don't understand. Why did Vita hold you captive?" Murphy asks.

"Vita knew the two of you would be connected." She squeezes my hand for reassurance. "She had her plan in effect even before Adria was born." Mared takes a deep breath before continuing. "Vita began coming to me in dreams, and I knew you were her target. I took you to Llyr who agreed to protect you and assured me that you would be raised by people who would love you."

"You helped me in the void. I remember your voice."

"Yes. I kept you alive as long as possible, and with the last of my power was able to separate your soul from your vessel and send it somewhere she couldn't find it."

Murphy sits heavily on the bench Bonnie and Sophie were in the process of rearranging. "I'm sorry, I don't know what to think."

"I understand," Mared answers. "I don't expect anything from you." She turns toward Bonnie. "Llyr kept his promise, and your family is perfect. Thank you, Bonnie, for being the mother I couldn't be."

Bonnie wipes a tear from her cheek. "Mared, you are a part of our family. We're the ones who owe you a thank you."

Murphy stands, moving in front of his birth mother. "Thank you, Mared. For saving my life—twice."

The five of us stare at each other in tears as Murphy wraps his arms around Mared, and the two of them embrace for the first time since he was an infant. Bonnie and Sophie join in the hug as the newly formed family cries and laughs together.

"What are we doing?" Ethan walks into the foyer, carrying a book.

Murphy pulls away from the group hug. "Dad, I'd like to introduce you to Mared, my birth mother."

Ethan doesn't hesitate. He wraps his arms around his wife and daughter, and the group joins together again.

Several minutes pass before Murphy steps away and moves back to my side. "Stephen and Rhys have created a meal that smells divine. I don't know about you all, but I'm starving. Will you join us, Mared?"

"I would like that, thank you." She follows our small group into the dining room. Murphy was right. The table is covered with enough food to feed an army. Keegan flashes a smile at Sophie as we enter.

"There you all are. I was going to start without you." He stands, pulling the chair next to him out and directing Sophie to sit.

"Who's this?" Brenna asks, entering the room.

"Brenna, this is Mared. She's my birth mother," Murphy answers.

"I believe we've met," Brenna says, stepping in front of the siren. "I recognize your energy. You saved my life in Greece." Brenna wraps her arms around the tall woman. "Thank you." Watching the two of them embrace brings more tears to my already weepy eyes. "You're Murphy's mother?" Mared nods. "I'm going to need more explanation later." The group laughs as we sit for a meal as a family.

"I'm not hungry, but I would enjoy the company. I

haven't had many conversations over the last few years," Mared says, moving toward an empty seat. Tempest enters the dining room and stops dead in his tracks.

"Hello," his deep voice rumbles through the room, and his face resembles a love-struck teenager as he stares at the beautiful siren.

I look between the two of them, feeling the energy radiate. "Tempest, this is Mared."

"It's a pleasure to meet you, Tempest," Mared says, as she moves toward him. "I haven't seen another water elemental for a very long time."

Tempest looks awkward as he stares blankly. The energy between them is electric and fills every corner of the room. Keegan claps his hands, interrupting the awkwardness. "Okay, how about some food?"

Tempest clears his throat. "Yes, I think that's a good idea." He pulls a chair away from the table, mirroring Keegan's move from earlier. "Please," he motions to the empty chair. "I would be honored to sit next to you." I've never seen Tempest like this, and it's strangely entertaining. I hope he doesn't discover he's flirting with one of his best friend's mother for at least a day or two. It's more entertaining that way.

"What?" Murphy asks, noticing the smirk on my face.

"Nothing." Looking around the large table, I don't miss the fact that I'm surrounded by my new family. Keegan and Sophie have their chairs so close together, there's barely any separation between the two. Tempest and Mared haven't stopped talking since our meal began, and the pointless banter around the table warms my heart.

I stand, knocking my chair over by accident, and the

room goes silent. "I didn't mean to make a scene." I laugh, awkwardly. "I just wanted to tell you all, thank you. Each one of you has meant more to me than I'm capable of expressing." I pause. "I've never been great with words." Murphy laces his fingers through mine, and I'm grateful for the touch. "Thank you for your support, for your love, and for being my friends."

Keegan is the first to his feet. He raises his wine glass high in the air. "To Adria, our fearless leader. I think I can speak for everyone in this room when I say we will follow you anywhere."

"Here, here," the rest of the table echoes, clinking their glasses together.

CHAPTER 21

"*I*t's been three months, Murphy. Your sister is old enough to make her own decisions about who she wants to date."

"Aye, I agree. But Keegan?"

I stifle a laugh. "Keegan has his quirks, but I trust him with my life. He's honest, hard-working, brilliant, and loyal. He makes the perfect mate for Sophie."

"Gods, do you have to use the word mate? That makes it sound even more perverse in my mind." He physically cringes. Murphy fills a small suitcase with the last of his clothes, looking around the red bedroom suite at the fire castle. "I'm ready to get back to the Isle."

I sigh. "Me too. Have you heard anything from your parents? Did they get back alright?"

"Aye, Mom said they arrived a few days ago and the bookstore was still standing." I laugh at his words.

"After all the books Ethan explored while here and at

Grimsgil, the bookstore will feel like a day at a county fair compared to spending a month at Disney."

Murphy laughs, "Knowing Dad, he snagged enough reading material from both libraries that he'll stay busy for at least a few months."

I shove a few of my favorite pairs of leggings into my small suitcase. The castle on the Isle of Man has a fully stocked closet, courtesy of Stephen. I don't need to take anything with me, but I can't leave my favorite brand here. Plus, you can never have too many pairs of leggings.

"Daniel just landed. If you're ready, I'll drive you both to the airport," Rhys announces as we reach the bottom of the stairs.

"That would be perfect, thank you." Rhys reaches for my bag as Brenna walks into the foyer.

"This feels familiar." She laughs.

"This time won't end the same way. You will be safe. I'll make sure of it."

Brenna wraps her arms around me. "We're not worried." She pulls away. "I'm going to miss all the noise around here. I've gotten used to having you kids around."

"Take care of each other. I'm leaving you in charge of the fire kingdom."

Brenna bows. "It will be my honor, Your Highness." I return her smile and follow Rhys to the SUV. It doesn't take long before we arrive at the airport. Like always, the *Smith Industries* jet is waiting on the tarmac. Rhys pulls the truck next to the stairs, and we unload straight into the plane.

"Welcome aboard," Keegan says, walking down the aisle.

"Are you taking my job now?" Sophie teases as she follows close behind.

"I wouldn't dream of it." He kisses her on the forehead.

Murphy clears his throat loudly. "Why are you here, Keegan?"

"I missed you guys!" he answers, patting Murphy on the shoulders. "Plus, Stephen asked me to pick you up at the airport."

"We missed you, too," I answer for the both of us. "Although, I'm thinking that Stephen meant for you to pick us up at the Isle of Man airport, not fly to Iceland to pick us up."

Keegan stares at me blankly. Clearly, the thought never crossed his mind. "I bet you're right," he answers, scratching his head. "But I did miss you guys."

"I thought you came to keep me company," Sophie says, ruffling Keegan's coal black hair.

"That too." He smiles, smoothing his hair back in place.

Our flight is quick and easy. Both Murphy and I fall asleep almost as soon as the jet lifts into the sky. The lull of Sophie and Keegan's soft flirtation plays in the back of my mind as I drift off to sleep.

"Adria?" Murphy's voice wakes me. "We're here."

My eyes open to see the familiar horizon from the jet window. "Did I sleep the entire flight?"

"Aye. You must have been tired." Truth is, I haven't been sleeping well since absorbing Vita's power. Between nursing Murphy back to health, and the craziness that has become my life, my mind is too busy to rest.

"I guess I was." I return the smile. Stepping off the jet, Stephen is parked at the bottom of the stairs, leaning against the black SUV.

"Keegan?" he says as we approach the truck. "Did you fly to Iceland to pick them up?"

"Maybe?" Keegan answers as Stephen rolls his eyes.

"Your Highness." Stephen turns his attention to me. "It's a pleasure to see you again."

I hug him. "Thank you, Stephen. It's wonderful to see you and to be home again." The butler blushes.

"I believe there's something at the castle that you will appreciate." He takes my bag, loading it in the back.

"For me? What is it?" I ask, not sure what's waiting for me.

"Shall we?" he says, opening the door for me. Murphy laughs at his lack of an answer. As we drive past the crystal clear sea into the village, the comfort of familiarity floods me. This is my home. This was Llyr's home. This is where I belong.

We cross the small bridge onto the island that holds the castle. A car sitting in front of the entrance grabs my attention immediately. "Who's here?" I ask Stephen.

"No one, ma'am. Just the usual."

"Whose car is that?" He doesn't answer as we pull alongside the vintage, bright red 1989 Ferrari. "That's a Testarossa." My car fangirl takes over, and I climb out of the truck before we fully stop.

In front of me sits my '80s dream car, in immaculate condition. I rub my hand across the fender, admiring the beauty of the build. I turn to see everyone's out of the

SUV and staring at me. "Seriously, Stephen. Whose car is this?"

Stephen holds up a key. "It's yours, Adria."

"What?" I turn to the car. "This is one of my dream cars. When I was a kid, I searched all over the city of L.A. for one to 'borrow' and could never find one from this year." I'm at a loss for words. "Did you do this?"

Stephen smiles proudly. "I did. I had a little help. Ethan helped me research, and we came up with this one. It doesn't replace the cars that were destroyed, but it's a start." I take the keys from his hand.

"This is perfect." Turning the key in the engine, it roars to life. It still smells like leather. After thirty-five years, it still smells like freaking leather.

"I'll take your bag inside," Murphy says. "Why don't you take it for a spin?" I don't hesitate to take him up on the offer. I pull away from my entourage, over the bridge, and past the village to where the roads are clear and open. Driving this car on my ancestral island brings the reality of life crashing down.

I've come full circle. From a kid stealing cars and homeless to the daughter of a god, my life has turned in directions I never thought possible. I downshift, pushing the car to speeds well over a hundred. The north point of the island comes into view, and I drift the rear end around a small curve. The car comes to a stop with little exertion.

I climb to the top of a large boulder and look over the sea. Waves assault the rocks below as the wind blows my hair relentlessly around my face. "I miss you!" I shout over the roar. "I miss you so damn much!"

The sky turns to midnight in an instant. The rocks

and sea that surrounded me disappear into complete blackness. "Seriously," I whisper. "What now?"

"I miss you too," my father's familiar voice says, echoing across the blackness of the void. I turn toward his voice, not sure if he's real.

"Llyr?"

"I'm here." He moves within feet of me and wipes a tear from my cheek. He's wearing blue jeans and a button-down shirt, turned up at the sleeves.

"You look...wonderful."

He laughs. "Death's been good to me." He motions behind him. "Someone else is here." Claire steps beside him.

"Mom?" I move closer, wrapping an arm around each of them. "Gods, I miss you both."

"We miss you, too," Claire echoes Llyr's words from earlier.

"You did good, kid," Llyr says, pulling away from our hug.

I huff a laugh. "I don't know about that."

"What happened was meant to be. Fate can be a bitch."

"I feel so...alone." I feel guilty even saying those words. It wasn't their choice to leave.

"You're not alone." Claire steps away. "We're here whenever you need us."

"And, you have Shu," Llyr adds.

I cross my arms over my chest. "Shu left."

"You know where to find him," Claire scolds.

"You can't expect me to be the one to make amends. You don't know what he's done."

She smiles. "You're right, I don't. But I do know you need each other, and he's all that's left of your family in this realm. Don't throw that away." Thoughts of my last words to him play through my mind, along with the pain those words caused.

"Shu has a shitty way of showing it, but he loves you, Adria. Don't ever doubt that. No matter what he's done, he did it out of his skewed perspective of love. Give him a little credit." Llyr's words strike deep.

"We have to go," Claire says as the two of them step back. "We're here when you need us. Just call on us like you did this time."

"Is that what I did?"

Llyr smiles. "Yes."

"I love you both." I wipe a tear.

"We love you," they say in unison.

"Go to Shu," Llyr adds before disappearing.

Blue returns to the sky, and the sea continues its assault on the rocks below. The bright red Ferrari is right where I left it, waiting patiently for my return. I breathe deeply, absorbing the sea air. "Okay," I say into the sky.

I push the Ferrari to speeds way too fast for an island road, but the freedom that comes from driving it releases the tension I've carried since this whole shit show started. I slow down to a respectable speed as I enter the village. The amount of people going on with their daily lives brings a smile to my face.

I park the car in front of the castle and hug it before going inside. Murphy, Keegan, and Sophie are sitting in the study, laughing about something as I enter.

"How was it?" Murphy asks.

"Amazing! It helped clear my mind about a few things." I sit next to him on the overstuffed chair. "I need to see Shu."

"Aye, I'll go with you."

"No. This is something I need to do alone." Murphy doesn't question me. He doesn't know what went on between the two of us but trusts me to know what's right. "I don't know when I'll get back." He laces his fingers through mine, kissing our joined hands.

"I'll be here when you do." I jump from the Isle and straight to the front door of Shu's house, where I met Tucker months ago.

"Adria? Is that you?" Tucker asks, coming up behind me. I turn, facing him. "It is you!" He moves in front of me quickly, wrapping his arms around me. "It's so good to see you!" He's wearing pretty much the same outfit as last time.

"It's good to see you again, Tucker."

"As much as I would like to think you're here to see me, I imagine you're here to see Shu." I don't answer. "He's been an insufferable ass for the past few months. Maybe you can do something with him."

"How is that different from normal?"

Tucker laughs. "True, but worse than normal." He opens the front door. "Please, come in. I'll make some tea." He nods his head toward a room off of the main living area. "He's in the sunroom. Good luck, you'll need it." He heads toward the kitchen.

I stand in the doorway, staring at the back of Shu's head, not sure what to say or how to even begin. "I know you're here. I sensed you the moment you arrived on the island."

"Tucker's right. You are more of an ass than usual." I step to the side of the chair he's occupying. He's wearing a pale blue sweater and a pair of jeans. It takes my brain a moment to recognize that I'm looking at Shu. "What are you wearing?"

Shu sighs, looking at his wardrobe. "It's what I wear when I'm not the God of Air. Things aren't always what they seem, Adria. I would think you of all people would know that by now."

"So, when you're here with Tucker you wear...colors?"

"When I'm here with Tucker, I can be myself. I don't have to be what or who everyone thinks I am. I can be me. Shu, the ass."

"I'm sure Tucker appreciates that." My words make him snicker.

"Why are you here? I distinctly remember you asking me why Llyr had to be the one to die while I got to live." He pauses. "I took that to mean you didn't want anything to do with me."

I sit in a chair opposite his. "I'm sorry I said that."

"You shouldn't be," he interrupts. "I've wondered the same thing since it happened. Why was he the one who died? I'm a horrible person. A horrible First. I've hurt so many people over the millennia, I've lost count. You were right to wonder why him and not me. If I could change that day, I would."

"Look at me," I demand of my grandfather. He reluctantly looks me in the eyes. "You are here because you're supposed to be here. Llyr's gone because he's supposed to be gone. What I said was wrong. It was mean, and I was trying to hurt you." He doesn't respond. "I knew it hurt you when I said it, and I'm sorry for that."

"Don't apologize. I deserved it."

"No, you didn't. You were only doing what you thought was the best for me and the cause. However skewed your process was, you were trying to make the right choice." Shu relaxes his shoulders at my words. "I forgive you, and I love you." Shu's energy changes the instant I utter those words.

"I love you, too," he echoes. "And, for what it's worth, I'm sorry."

I smile. "It's not worth much."

"Touché," he answers with a matching smile.

"I have tea," Tucker announces in a singsong voice from the living room. "Come get it before it gets cold."

"He's a stickler about hot tea. We better listen."

"There's something we need to do first." I stick my head into the living room. "I need to borrow Shu for a few minutes. Can you keep it warm?"

"For you, anything." Tucker smiles a toothy grin. I grab Shu's hand and jump both of us to a familiar beach on the coast of California.

"Adria? Why are we here?" Shu walks around the empty beach, moving close to the water's edge.

"This is where she died."

"I don't want to be here."

"I know you don't, but you need to be here." I take his hand into mine. "You need to let her go."

"I never had her *to* let go." His voice sounds sadder than I've ever heard it.

"That's true, but when you found out she existed and was already gone, you did everything in your power to hurt those around you like you'd been hurt."

Shu looks at our joined hands. "You and Llyr."

"Not just us. Everyone. This persona you play of the god that dresses in all white and sequins, it's all part of a character you play. I love the real you. The one who married a human lumberjack who makes tea and gets pissed when it gets cold. The one who wears blue when no one can see him. This is the real you, Shu."

Shu's voice breaks when he speaks. "How'd you turn out to be so amazing?"

"Good genes." I laugh. We both look over the calm sea. "Tell her goodbye. She'll hear you."

Shu waits so long that I'm convinced he's ignoring my request. "Goodbye, my sweet, sweet girl. I regret we never had the opportunity to meet. I will love you for all of this life and beyond. Thank you for giving me the most amazing blessing of your daughter." His words bring tears to my eyes.

EPILOGUE

"*A*dria, be still. I can't fit this dress to you with you wiggling around." Sophie tugs the fabric, pulling it tighter than necessary. "Don't breathe, I almost have the last pin in."

"If I didn't know better, I'd think you were trying to kill me."

"You've figured me out. After five years of knowing you, I've decided to stab the Goddess of All Elements with a straight pin, in hopes it will kill her." Her voice is monotone, making me giggle at her words.

"If the straight pin doesn't do it, the lack of being able to breathe surely will."

"Got it! Look in the mirror." Sophie stands back proudly, putting her hands on her hips. I turn facing the oversized mirror, and for the first time in a while, I'm speechless. "See!" she says, punching my shoulder.

"Sophie, I...I don't know what to say. It's beautiful. You do amazing work."

She smiles, trying not to look boastful. "Thank you. Being a fashion designer is something I've wanted to do my entire life. I don't know what took me so long to get here."

"You just needed a little...encouragement."

"Is that what we're calling it now? Encouragement?" she scoffs.

I face her. "As long as you were working for *Smith Industries*, you weren't pursuing your dreams. Making you my personal designer was the only way to get you to chase your dreams."

"Well, the huge raise that came with the position helped. As much as it pains me to admit it, you were right."

I pretend to have a heart attack. "What did you just say? Did I hear that correctly?"

"Now, you'll never hear it again. If you mess up that dress, I'll stab you with a straight pin, Goddess or not."

"Did I just hear you threatening Adria?" Murphy asks, entering the room.

"Aye, and if she messes this dress up before I get it finished, I will follow through on my threat." Sophie crosses her arms over her chest.

"You might want to be careful, Adria. I've seen what she's capable of." Murphy points to a tiny scar on the tip of his nose. "See this?" I squint trying to see what he's pointing at. "This is what I like to call the Lego incident of twenty-ten."

Sophie holds her hands up in surrender style. "You stole my creation and told Mom you made it yourself! What did you expect?"

"Point taken. Sophie, can you help me out of the dress? I don't want a twin to Murphy's scar." She scoffs, moving behind me to remove pins.

"That dress is beautiful, Sophie. Adria will be the center of attention."

"Yay, you know how much I love getting all the attention." My tone is full of sarcasm.

"Get out, unless you want to see her boobs," Sophie announces as she's about to pull the last pin.

"In that case." Murphy sits on the couch in my room.

"Get out!" Sophie shouts playfully while throwing a pillow at him. He jumps to his feet and follows orders. "I love my brother, but I want to hurt him sometimes." Sophie carries the bundle of aqua taffeta that will be my dress to the bed.

"I never had a brother, but I imagine that's the sentiment of most sisters."

"Aye. I'll finish the dress and have it ready in plenty of time for the wedding." She carries the bundle of fabric to the door. "Adria, thank you for giving me this opportunity."

"You don't have to thank me. I think of you as my best friend, and no one deserves the recognition more than you."

"Don't make me cry," she says, exiting the door.

"I saw a huge wad of fabric heading down the hallway, so I assumed it was safe to come back," Murphy says, coming back into the room. He moves behind me quickly, wrapping his arms around my waist and pulling me close. "Gods, you smell good."

"Thank you. It's soap." He laughs, kissing my neck

just below my earlobe. "Don't start something we don't have time to finish."

"Can't you call the Time Goddess from the seventh realm and ask her for an extra thirty minutes?" He continues his assault on my neck.

"As tempting as that is, Mira has enough to deal with in her own realm. Giving us an extra few minutes is not at the top of her list." A loud knock on the door stops both of us in our tracks.

"Excuse me, Adria. Several of the overnight guests have begun arriving for the wedding. I thought you might want to greet them," Stephen calls through the door.

"She's busy," Murphy answers.

"Stop," I whisper before clearing my throat. "Thank you, Stephen. We'll be right there."

"He's a pain in the ass sometimes," Murphy whispers.

"Aren't we all?" I turn to face the man I love and wrap my arms completely around him, pulling him as close as possible. "We will finish this later. Tonight is for wedding guests."

"Aye, to later." His lips are on mine in an instant and heat rises from my core. Over the past five years, we've kissed countless times. The intensity and heat that passes between us are as strong as the first kiss we shared that night on the bridge. In a matter of seconds, both of us are breathing harder than necessary. "We better go. I'm not going to be able to stop if this goes on any longer."

I take a step back, placing my hands on his cheeks. "I love you, Murphy Aloysius McKenzie."

"I love you, Adria Kane Smith McKenzie." He holds his arm out, and I wrap mine through as we exit our shared room toward the landing and the noise of the guests below. I feel a familiar energy the moment we reach the top of the stairs.

"Shu's here!" I run down the stairs, taking them two at a time, with Murphy right on my heels. I follow his energy to the study to find my grandfather, wearing a pair of navy dress pants, a blue button-down silk shirt, and black shoes. Standing beside him is Tucker, wearing his usual lumberjack gear. I rush the two of them, wrapping an arm around each. "Oh, my gods. I've missed you both."

"Adria!" Tucker says, wiping a tear. "We've missed seeing you the past few months."

"I'm sorry I haven't visited more. I've been so busy traveling through the realms, I haven't had much time for my own."

"Oh, you're forgiven, my dear." Shu raises his signature glass of brandy as a toast. "Well, look who the cat dragged in." Shu drinks the entire glass of brandy as Brenna and Rhys enter the room.

"What happened to you?" Brenna asks. "Did you get attacked by a smurf? I've never seen you wear anything but white."

Shu pours another glass. "Think of it as my coming out party."

Brenna laughs. "You came out millennia ago. It's a little late to throw a party now."

"I like her," Tucker says, holding his hand toward Brenna. She shakes it with a smile. "I'm Tucker, Shu's husband."

It takes a moment for her to process his words. "Bless your heart." Brenna moves to the brandy cart. "Let me get you something to drink. I'm sure you need it." Tucker laughs and accepts her offer.

"Brenna, Rhys, I'm so glad you two could make it to the wedding." I give her a tight squeeze.

"We wouldn't have missed it for the world," Rhys says, hugging me from the other side.

"Where's my boy?" Brenna asks, looking around the room.

"Probably hanging out with the groomsmen," Murphy answers. "I'll go let him know you're here."

"That's not necessary." Brenna stands very still, and I feel a blast of energy leave her body. "He'll be here shortly."

"Did you just call him with energy?"

Before she can answer, Keegan bursts into the room. "Brenna!" He rushes her, picks her small body up, and spins her around like she's a child. "I've missed you so much!"

Brenna's laughter fills the room. "I've missed you too, my boy. Put me down so I can get a look at you." He follows directions. She looks him up and down. "You look good. Love has been good for you."

"You too," Keegan answers as he shakes Rhys's hand. "Thank you for taking care of her."

"I think that's backward," Rhys laughs. "She takes care of me."

"We take care of each other," Brenna adds. "Where is your love?"

Keegan looks around the room. "To be honest, I'm not sure."

"Oh, she's finishing up my dress for tomorrow. She

insisted on making it. Wait until you see it. It's the most beautiful creation I've ever had the pleasure of wearing."

"I don't doubt it," Keegan answers. "Would you like to see where the ceremony is going to take place?" he asks the room.

"Why not?" Shu says, finishing probably his third glass of brandy. Tucker taps him on the shoulder, shooting him an ugly look, and I can't help but laugh. Tucker is reprimanding the God of Air for being an asshole. Shu shrugs, putting down his glass, and follows the small crowd to the back veranda.

Below, we can see the beach and the decorations waiting to be put out. Although completely capable of doing it himself, Stephen hired people to do the work. His one request of me was to stop any element that might cause havoc on the wedding. The normally windy beach is calm and perfect for the upcoming nuptials.

"Those flower arrangements are to die for. This is going to be a beautiful wedding." Tucker's excitement warms my heart. "Is there anything I need to do to help?"

"I believe they have everything under control," Stephen answers. "If you'll follow me inside, dinner is ready."

"Oh, thank gods. I'm starved," Keegan announces, leading the pack.

"Me too." Murphy's right behind him. The large dining table is set with the finest crystal we have to offer. Fresh roses and gardenias take up residence in the center of the table. Their fragrance fills the room with love.

"Is there room for two more?" A deep voice asks, coming into the room.

"Tempest!" I jump in front of him and wrap my arms around his neck. "It's so good to see you."

"As it is you, Your Highness." I turn to the beautiful siren beside him.

"Mared, you look breathtaking. It's wonderful to see you both." She smiles, hugging me tightly.

"Thank you, dear. I owe everything to you." She turns to Murphy. "It's good to see you again."

"Aye, you too." He pulls her into a tight hug. "Adria's right. You look beautiful."

"As do you." She smiles.

Keegan doesn't say a word. Just walks over to Tempest and wraps his arms around him. "I've missed you too, little man," Tempest says, pulling away from their embrace. "You look good. Love's been good to you."

"Hah, I told you so." Brenna laughs. "Go get that girl of yours so we can eat."

"I'll go," I volunteer. "I know where she is." I jump to the sewing room she's created in one of the lesser-used wings. The walls are covered in pale blue wallpaper, and the wooden floors are covered in what looks like pieces of my dress and thread. She's bent over a sewing machine, carefully guiding the needle through the fabric. "Hey," I say.

"Holy shit!" Sophie exclaims, jumping off the antique bench. "What the hell, Adria?"

I can't hold in my laugh. "I didn't mean to scare you." Sophie walks around with her hand on her heart. "How's the dress coming?"

"Well, before you scared the shit out of me, I was finishing the zipper." She moves to the pile of fabric that's not covering the floor. She holds it up in front of her. "What do you think?"

"Sophie, it's absolutely stunning. I can't wait to wear it." She smiles. "I have a few sequins I want to add to the front, but that won't take long."

"Can you take a break for food?"

"Is that even a question?" She laughs. "We McKenzie's do enjoy eating."

"There she is!" Keegan says as we enter the room. He escorts her to the table, pulling her chair out for her.

I look around the room at my family—one by blood, the rest by love. The conversation is light and comfortable as we eat our meal, enjoying each other's company. This is what I've wanted my entire life. Family isn't just something you're born into. It's something you make and surround yourself with.

......

Cloudless blue skies, seventy-degree temperatures, and calm seas are the perfect backdrop for a once in a lifetime wedding. Guests from the village and the sea have been arriving for the past few hours and mingling with each other around the catered meal. I'm waiting until the last possible moment to change into the dress Sophie made. For now, I'm wearing a fitted suit, the same color as the dress. Sophie designed this for me too, but it's not as elaborate as the dress I'll wear later.

"Adria, it's time to change." Sophie wraps her arm through mine, dragging me into the castle. "I'll help you zip it." My hair and makeup are already done. It doesn't take long to slip into the custom-fit dress. Sophie claps her hands. "It's perfect!"

"Your Highness," Tempest says, meeting us at the bottom of the stairs. He's dressed in a tuxedo with a bowtie and cummerbund that matches my dress. His yellow-blonde hair is slicked back and has grown so long it's tied into a low bun.

"Tempest, you look...you look handsome," I stumble over my words.

He smiles. "Thank you, Highness." He offers his arm to me. "Ready?" I wrap my arm through his and the two of us exit the back door and move to where the guests are waiting. The beach is lined with water elementals, while earth and air elementals attend from below and above. All are disguised into their surroundings. We take our places at the front of the audience, him on one side and me in the middle.

A string trio begins to play the traditional wedding song as Mared, escorted by Murphy, makes her way down the aisle. She's wearing a stunningly beautiful off-white gown that hugs her hips and accentuates her figure in all the right places. Her blue skin has transformed into human hues, disguising her true identity from the non-elementals in attendance. Auburn red hair cascades down her back and is held together with a small grouping of flowers and seashells. "She's beautiful," I whisper to my friend. "Congratulations."

"That she is," he answers. Murphy stops in front of me with the beautiful siren on his arm. He winks and flashes a smile that's meant only for me.

"Who gives this woman to be married today?" I smile at my words.

"I do," Murphy answers. "Her son." He reaches over, kissing her on the cheek. "Take care of her, stepdaddy." He unwraps Mared's arm from his and hands it to Tempest. The fact that Tempest will now officially be Murphy's stepfather has eluded me until this moment.

Vows are exchanged and promises are made as I join Tempest and Mared in the sacred bond of marriage.

"With the power vested in me by...by the Isle of Man, I now pronounce you man and wife. Tempest, you may now kiss your bride."

ACKNOWLEDGMENTS

Stephanie-who would have thought that meeting you on a random Facebook site would turn into the best book friend I have? You've been an amazing alpha and beta reader, as well as the comma queen and my sounding board. Thank you for encouraging me to publish on my own. Without you, I wouldn't have taken the plunge.

Elizabeth, I'm so glad I found you! You are an amazing proofreader. When you get famous, don't forget about me.

To my husband and children who refuse to read anything I write. Don't expect anything for Christmas. (Just kidding... maybe)

ABOUT THE AUTHOR

Madalyn Rae is the pen name for an author who loves telling a story. As a teacher of tiny humans during the day and author by night, she hopes she's able to draw you into her world of fantasy, make-believe, and love, even for a brief moment.

She lives on the beautiful white, sandy beaches of the Gulf Coast, with her husband and two loyal, yet mildly obnoxious dogs, Whiskey and Tippi. She's the mother of two amazing adult children and a brand new son-in-law.

When not teaching or pretending to write, Madalyn is immersed in the world of music. Whether playing an instrument or singing a song, she is privileged to know that music is the true magic of the universe.

Coming Soon-
"Vampires of New Orleans" 2023-2024.
"Ravenwood"-2024 *A Vampire of New Orleans Spin-off*

ALSO BY MADALYN RAE

The Elementals Series

Birth of the Phoenix-Adria's Novella-Prequel

Phoenix of the Sea- Elementals Book 1

Guardian of the Sea- Murphy's Novella

Ashes of the Wind-Elementals Book 2

Embers of the Flame-Keegan's Novella

Fire of the Sky-Elementals Book 3

Vampires of New Orleans Series

Garden of the Past-Origin Novella Prequel-Fall 2023

Garden of Secret and Shadow-Book 1-Fall 2023

Garden of Mystery and Intrigue (Working Title)-Book 2-

Winter 2023

Garden of Discovery and Love- (Working Title)

Winter 2024

Ravenwood-VONO Spin-Off

Spring 2024

Printed in Great Britain
by Amazon